AR Quiz#: 102141
BL: 5.5
AR Pts: 6.0

# FIRST BOY

# GARY SCHMIDT

★ ★ ★ ★ ★ ★ ★ ★ ★ ★

# FIRST
# BOY

★ ★ ★ ★ ★ ★ ★ ★ ★ ★

SQUARE
FISH

HENRY HOLT AND COMPANY

SQUARE
FISH

An Imprint of Holtzbrinck Publishers

Square Fish and the Square Fish logo are trademarks of Holtzbrinck Publishers, LLC and are used
by Henry Holt and Company under license from Holtzbrinck Publishers, LLC.

Library of Congress Cataloging-in-Publication Data
Schmidt, Gary D.
First boy / Gary Schmidt.—1st ed.
p.     cm.
Summary: Dragged into the political turmoil of a presidential election
year, fourteen-year-old Cooper Jewett, who runs a New Hampshire
dairy farm since his grandfather's death, stands up for himself and
makes it clear whose first boy he really is.
[1. Dairy farming—Fiction.    2. Farm life—Fiction.    3. Elections—Fiction.
4. Presidents—Family—Fiction.    5. New Hampshire—Fiction.]    I. Title.
PZ7.S3527Fi 2005        [Fic]—dc22        2004060747

ISBN-13: 978-0-312-37149-4 / ISBN-10: 0-312-37149-7

Originally published in the United States by Henry Holt and Company, LLC
Designed by Patrick Collins
First Square Fish Edition: September 2007
10  9  8  7  6  5  4  3  2  1
www.squarefishbooks.com

All the political chicanery, for James;

All the moments between Mr. Searle
and Mrs. Perley on the porch stoop, for Kathleen;

All the lovely autumn fields of New England, for Rebecca;

All the mayhem, for David;

All the peace and tranquillity, for Margaret;

All the tractors and patrol cars and jeeps and Plymouths
and black sedans, for Benjamin;

And all the rest for you too, you who are my best poetry

# CONTENTS

# FIRST BOY

★ ★ ★ ★ ★ ★ ★ ★ ★

## CHAPTER ONE

PETER HURD saw the black sedan first—dark and slow, prowling Main Street like a panther. It stopped beside the granite steps of New Lincoln Public Library as if to look for prey. Then it came on again, still slow, low to the ground. It paused by the Miracle Theatre, and by the New Lincoln Diner, and then right beside New Lincoln Market—right beside Peter—where it crouched and waited. Its windows were tinted so deeply that Peter couldn't see inside at all.

"Jewett," Peter called back into the market.

Cooper Jewett wasn't in any hurry to come outside. They had just finished freshman cross practice, and Cooper was savoring the last few swallows of his forbidden root beer. Coach would take him apart if he knew that Cooper was drinking anything but water. "Soda will kill you. It'll send little carbonated bubbles right through your bloodstream and up into your heart. Then they'll all come together and bust." Coach would throw his arms up in an explosion. "Soda will kill you, just like that."

But after a run on a September afternoon that could still hold an August heat, Cooper and Peter generally decided that an icy Admiral Ames Root Beer was worth the risk.

"Jewett," Peter called again.

Cooper took another cold swallow.

The black sedan moved on. Peter watched it stalk off Main Street and down onto Whittier Road. He realized that he had been holding his breath.

Cooper came out, Admiral Ames Root Beer still sweet on his lips. "I've got the flour and sugar," he said. "You get the milk."

Peter took the milk Cooper handed to him, his eyes still watching the corner.

Cooper got on his bike and hunched his loaded backpack up around his shoulders. "If Old Ford was here, I could drive us home," he said.

"Could you drive a sedan?"

"I guess. If it had a stick."

"Maybe you'll get your chance."

Cooper looked at him. Sometimes Hurd could say crazy things like that, out of the blue. "You think a sedan is going to stop and ask us in so we can drive home?"

"Why not?"

"Because this is New Lincoln, New Hampshire, and the only strange thing around here is you."

"Witty," said Peter. "Very witty." He hauled the milk on top of his handlebars and pushed off. Cooper pushed off too, the flour and sugar heavy in his backpack, and side by side they rode down Main Street, past Whittier, and so out of town.

The last strong heat of the day laid its hand on Cooper as he pedaled, but it felt good to him. Cross practice had been a nine-mile run—four of them at race pace—and for all but the last two miles he had kept up with Peter. He felt his muscles tighten and relax, tighten and relax with the pedals, with no sign of little carbonated bubbles rushing toward a bust in his heart. He shifted his pack as his front wheel left the pavement at the end of Main Street and looked for a smooth run on the dirt road that led to Hurd's house. His drive waited at the bottom of a long hill, and they could coast all the way, fast enough to hear the spokes whistle, and then cut in at the last second where Hurd's brothers had built up the bank.

But at the bottom, Peter didn't cut in at the last second. He braked and slid his back tire out to the front, looking up at the top of the next hill ahead. Cooper braked right behind him.

A black sedan crouched, its brake lights bright.

"Jewett, I saw a sedan in town."

The brake lights dimmed, and the sedan moved smoothly over the arch of the hill.

"Now you saw one out of town," said Cooper.

Peter stared at him. "Don't you want to know what two cars like that are doing in New Lincoln?"

Cooper shrugged. "If they were Fords, maybe. If they were Ford pickups, say, 1958 or '59, then I'd care."

"Jewett, you should wonder if there's something wrong with you. No one else in the state wants to drive a fifty-year-old pickup."

"I think of myself as unique, individual, independent, one of a kind, a freethinker," said Cooper.

"There's something wrong with you," said Peter, and they biked up to the Hurd house.

It was a long drive to a small farmhouse, and Cooper sometimes wondered how it was that all the Hurds could fit inside at once. Maybe they couldn't. There was a Hurd in every single grade from New Lincoln Elementary to New Lincoln High, and two in eighth grade, and three in first, and one off to college. Between them all, they could almost field both sides of a baseball game, except the roster would be dang hard to keep straight, and who could call the game with all those Hurds?

*Hurd up, with two outs. Hurd with two strikes and a ball. Hurd winds up. Hurd on first leads, held on by Hurd. Hurd pitches, and Hurd swings, and Hurd takes off for second. Hurd tracks it down in center . . .*

★ 6 ★

★ ★ ★

Mrs. Hurd, surrounded by a good part of her roster, was waiting for them on the front steps. She took the flour and sugar from Cooper and handed them to a young Hurd, took the milk from Peter and handed it to another young Hurd, gave Cooper a brownie—her hands moved as quickly as a bird's wing—and gave another to Peter. "Eat them now," she said, and fluttered inside.

Cooper ate his now, but he wasn't finished before Mrs. Hurd was back out and handing him a basket—with a pie! An apple pie! One of Mrs. Hurd's apple pies!

"It has too much cinnamon in it," she said, "and I'm worried that the apples might be too tart—" one of Mrs. Hurd's prizewinning, blue-ribbon, best-in-the-state apple pies! "—and it's probably not baked enough. But it's about milking time, so you'd best get on home with it."

"See you, Jewett," said Peter, and Cooper watched him get swallowed up and become part of the Hurd nest of bustle and business. "There was this black sedan in town," Cooper heard him say, and then Peter was gone inside.

Cooper swung his bike out and headed home, balancing the pie in one hand, his mouth still full of brownie. He pumped hard down the drive and up the hill, his legs burning from cross practice—but still no little carbonated bubbles right through his bloodstream—reached the top, and coasted down toward the Jewett farm. The breeze chilled him, the wind sang again in his spokes, and the farm spread out below him, the cows already heading toward the barn. The cinnamon smell of the apple pie came up out of the basket.

And for a moment, it was all so right. For a moment. Then the stillness clutched him.

He wished he had a dog waiting for him—a retriever named Barkus. If there was a dog, they'd go on Saturdays to show off on New Lincoln Common, and together he and Barkus would be Frisbee champions of all New Hampshire.

He wished he had a brother or sister waiting. A brother to mess around with. Someone to do chores with. Someone on a lower bunk to talk to before he fell asleep at night.

He wished he had a mother and a father, waiting with brownies when he came home from cross practice. On weekends they would climb into a car that had a muffler and a back seat even, instead of Old Ford, and drive to his meets. They would keep his times, and cheer him through the sweat of the last quarter mile.

He wished—he could hardly let the thought come—he wished he had a grandmother. He did have one until a year ago. She'd cook one thing he really, really liked each night, so he could choke down the lima beans that were good for him because there were sweet potatoes crisped with brown sugar right beside them.

And he would tend her garden for her so that it would take more blue ribbons than a Fourth of July parade.

He still tended it. One more way to remember her.

But with the apple pie and its cinnamon smell, he was coasting down only to his grandfather, who liked to say, "There's no use wishing for what the good Lord isn't going to send you. You just have to make do." Cooper figured that this was so, and most days he tried to make do and not to wish. But after stopping at Hurd's house, trying not to wish was like the orange sun trying not to jump up to morning or the pastel moon trying not to glow at dusk.

So he did wish all down the hill. But he knew his grandfather was right: The good Lord had no intention of sending him anything he wished for.

Which is not to say Cooper wasn't happy. Every day he ran cross hard enough to ache his muscles, worked at chores long enough to fall asleep quick and easy, and loved his grandfather, his wiry, cantankerous New Hampshire dairyman grouse of a grandfather, enough to almost fill the hole in his heart.

So almost every day ended happy. Tuckered, but happy. And this one did too. Together Cooper and his grandfather finished chores and evening milking, ate supper and most of the apple pie, and put up the dishes. Cooper read Geometry, and his grandfather read Zane Grey. And when they had had enough of math and the

Old West, they ate the rest of the pie and then sat down in the parlor to watch the late news. Sort of.

What with morning milking, then hauling hay bales to the loft, then weeding carrots until breakfast, then New Lincoln High School, freshman cross, then more hay bales and carrots in the afternoon, then evening milking, by the time the late news came on, Cooper was about as tired as a boy could get. He was glad his grandfather wasn't one to talk. "Talk is only silence that ain't working well," his grandfather said. And most nights—tonight especially, somehow—Cooper was glad of good silence.

He yawned, then looked over at his grandfather watching the news. So still. So tuckered. He began to wonder if he was too still and too tuckered. Tuckered with the whole weary world. *Maybe,* thought Cooper, *maybe I should start taking on evening milking by myself.*

He stretched and felt his muscles tighten and ache across his back and up and down his legs. At fourteen, he was already bigger than his grandfather—not taller, but bigger—and he wondered for about the quadrillionth time where his looks came from. As far as he could tell, there wasn't another Jewett with hair this light and eyes this green. Not to mention these ears that stuck out farther than he wished they did.

The news droned on—nothing new, but Hannah Joyce, roving reporter, all excited about it.

He leaned closer to his quiet grandfather, and Cooper

wondered for about the octillionth time why he looked so different. And why he was the only kid on the continent who'd never seen a picture of his mother or father. Golly Moses, not one single picture.

When Hannah Joyce announced an interview with Senator Wickham and his voice began to pulpit forth from the screen, Cooper sat back. He knew his grandfather would wake up as excited as Hannah Joyce—because he loved hating politicians. Senators and representatives, governors and selectmen and mayors—there wasn't a one that he couldn't find good reason to hate. And among politicians as a group, there was none he could find more reasons to hate than Senator Wickham, who, he said, should hold a pile of manure in each hand while he talked so people could plainly see what was coming out of his mouth. (He never said this aloud in New Lincoln Methodist Church.)

"Our country needs to be heading in new directions. And to get to those new directions our country needs a new vision. And to get a new vision we need a new leader," Senator Wickham was saying.

Hannah Joyce tilted her head. "But isn't it unusual for a candidate to challenge a sitting president in a primary when both are in the same party? Some might say that you are doing harm to the Democrats, perhaps even threatening to split the vote when the national election begins."

"Some might say that," said Senator Wickham. "But not those who can see how out of touch this President has become. I've walked among the people of New Hampshire. I've heard their stories. I've eaten in their homes and gone with them to their jobs. And I know that the President of the United States is responsible for dealing with the bread-and-butter issues that affect the citizens of New Hampshire every day of their life. This President doesn't believe that. And that's why I'm challenging the sitting President of my own party."

Cooper's grandfather woke up. "A bunch of hooey," he said. "He's not even grammatical."

Smiling, Hannah Joyce tried to put on a serious frown to ask a thoughtful question. "What bread-and-butter issues exactly, Senator?"

"Family, for one. Despite campaign promises up and down and all across our country, this President has made no effort to support New England's families. This is something we should all consider carefully. Very carefully. The American people should almost wonder if there was cause for the President's abandonment of our families. In the bill that I propose for the relief of New Hampshire . . ."

"Good Lord," said Grandpa. He stood up and turned off the set. "That'll do for him tonight." He yawned, and his eyes drooped. Cooper figured he must be awful tired to miss a chance to hate Senator Wickham.

"As if he knew a single thing about New Hampshire families. As if he had one," said Grandpa.

*What is there to know about New Hampshire families?* thought Cooper. *Except some have a roster for theirs. Others have barely enough for Ping-Pong.*

His grandfather yawned again and rubbed his arm.

"You go on up, Grandpa," said Cooper. "I'll check everything tonight."

His grandfather nodded. "I guess I got a cold or something. I ache terrible."

"If Grandma were here, she'd give you a horehound to suck on."

"And hotten up a can of chicken soup."

"And put an afghan around your shoulders to keep you warm while you ate the soup."

"Yes, she would," he said. He walked over to her rocking chair and rubbed his fingers slowly along its top. "Well, you know what to do same as me." Then he came over to the couch and leaned over Cooper. "You're my first boy, Cooper, my first boy." Grandpa tousled his hair.

He had never done it before. His grandfather hardly ever touched him, him being a wiry, cantankerous New Hampshire dairyman grouse of a grandfather. Cooper felt his hand on him and heard his voice for the rest of that night and for many nights after that.

Cooper went out to check that the Small Barn was locked—it was—and that the cows in the Big Barn had settled down–they had. The Farmall wasn't backed under the shed, so he climbed up and turned the ignition and felt the thrill of the tractor under him as it grumbled and then woke up. He loved the roar of the machine, the smell of the combustion, the shuddering of the seat as the back wheels began to take the ground. His grandfather didn't care much for it at all, it being just a tractor. He used a cushion when he drove it. But Cooper didn't want anything between him and the machine. Riding that tractor with a load of hay from the Far Pasture, Cooper felt like he could drag up the whole landscape behind him if he had half a mind to.

He wondered for the trillionth time where that came from, since Grandpa said that Jewetts and machines weren't cozy together.

Back in the parlor he turned out the lights, then the ones in the hall. In the kitchen he left one on–Grandpa believed that all good New Hampshire dairymen needed something with lots of sugar in it sometime in the middle of the night. Then he headed up himself and, at the top of the stairs, paused to look out the window over the farm. Another day finished, and this one finished with his grandfather's voice: "You're my first boy, Cooper, my first boy."

He didn't know until morning that those were the last words he would hear his grandfather say.

Cooper thought of them when he found him, the first

time he'd ever known him to stay in bed after the orange sun had jumped up to morning. He thought of them while he waited hopelessly for Sheriff Gibbs. He thought of them while he stood on the clean white tiles of the emergency room and listened to the doctor explain. He thought of them while Reverend Hurd drove him back home to a house as empty as sorrow, his grandfather's watch in his hand. (He had never seen it off him before.)

He thought of them when Mrs. Perley, who lived in the house above Cooper, brought his supper down that night and stayed with him while he sat in the rocker and ate. He thought of them when Mr. Searle, who lived in the dairy farm below Cooper, came to help out at evening milking, and then again the next morning. He thought of them three days later while he sweated in the overheated funeral parlor. Grandpa could never stand a house too hot. And he thought of them at the service the next morning in New Lincoln Methodist, sitting surrounded by Hurds, all as quiet and still as could be, because who knew what to say to a kid with no dog, no brother or sister, no mother or father, no grandmother, no grandfather?

"You're my first boy, Cooper, my first boy."

Afterward, folks from church came back to the farm. Reverend Hurd prayed a prayer with "thee"s and "thou"s in it, and then folks started to "partake"—which was Reverend Hurd's word for "eat." Mrs. Perley had made more sandwiches, salads, and raspberry tarts than all New Lincoln could partake of. But Mr. Searle tried his hardest to make her come up short.

Everyone told Cooper that Eli Jewett had gone to his heavenly reward, that he was safe with Jesus, that he was with Edna again, that he was in a better place. But Cooper knew Jesus didn't need him, his grandmother would have waited, and his grandfather wouldn't find heaven so much better than the farm. What were Pearly Gates when he could open the Big Barn doors every morning and hear the warm, soft moos of cows waking up?

*Not much,* thought Cooper.

But he knew this: He would open those doors every day. He would hear the warm, soft moos. He would weed the carrots, and he would milk the cows, because this farm was all he had left. It felt like it was all he would ever have left.

There was quiet Methodist talk while the piles of Mrs. Perley's sandwiches and salads and raspberry tarts yielded to the partakers. And then the talk dwindled, and Cooper watched folks stretch out their collars and check their watches. John Hurd fussed because Dorcas Hurd took the last raspberry tart and he had wanted it and she had four already and he had only three and now it was too late because she had already licked it and wasn't it time for them to go yet?

It was, and one by one, the congregation of New Lincoln Methodist shook Cooper's hand and left. Each time someone stood on the top step of the porch, it groaned loudly, as if the house was mourning. When Peter punched him on the shoulder, then gathered the flock of Hurds and herded them home, Cooper's world got very still.

Then there was only Mrs. Hurd cleaning up with Mrs. Perley, and Reverend Hurd and Mr. Searle considering whether they should help—and deciding against it.

Then they were done. The kitchen clean. And nothing else to do but to make do.

"Cooper, is there someone to come for you?" asked Reverend Hurd.

Cooper looked at him. Deep down, there was something that had stopped in him. He felt it sprung and still. And whatever it was, he was afraid to even think about letting it start again. Because if he tried, golly Moses if he tried, he might discover that it had no reason to start again. And what would he do then?

"No one you know?" asked Reverend Hurd.

Cooper shook his head.

"Come stay with us. It would be a change for you, living in a crowd."

But Cooper shook his head again.

"You shouldn't stay here alone," said Mrs. Hurd. "You can bunk with Peter tonight, and we'll figure—"

"I can't leave," said Cooper. "It's my place now, and Grandpa would expect me to stay. I have to keep up."

"Boy all alone on a dairy farm this size, isn't possible you'll keep up," said Mr. Searle.

"I'll keep up," said Cooper.

Mr. Searle did not look like he believed he could. Reverend Hurd did not look like he believed he could.

"I figure my father had some uncles or something."

"Don't know of any," said Mr. Searle.

"I'll look in my grandfather's desk. There must be another Jewett somewhere in New Hampshire."

"I expect there is, but your father weren't a Jewett. Your mother either, far as I know."

"He had to be a Jewett. Golly Moses, I'm a Jewett."

"Hush, Searle, you old goat," said Mrs. Perley.

"Well, the boy's being so dang stubborn. He can't run a dairy farm alone, whoever he is."

"And you are Patience itself, are you not? Gracious goodness, he has enough to think about without your two cents' worth." Mrs. Perley turned to Cooper. "No one is going to take you out of your house, Cooper. You are a dairyman, just like Eli." Cooper nodded. "But we do not want you all alone, either. So I will stay the night, and the Old Grumpus will be up to help with chores in the morning."

"Don't know how long I can do that. I've got my own place to tend to."

"Until things settle down," said Mrs. Perley. "You have only a half-dozen cows in that big old barn. It is not as though you had an entire herd anymore."

"It hardly matters. They still need tending to, and even a mostly empty barn needs to be kept up."

"I can keep up," said Cooper.

Mr. Searle snorted. "Sure you can, boy, all by yourself."

"I don't need help," said Cooper.

Mr. Searle snorted again. He put his hat on and left. The top step groaned very loudly.

Even the bottom step groaned.

"I'll keep up," Cooper whispered after him.

Reverend Hurd shook his hand, and Mrs. Hurd gathered him in and put her arms around him like wings. They didn't say anything more. Maybe they too knew that talk could be silence that ain't working. They left to follow their flock.

So Mrs. Perley was the last to leave, the last one to pat him on the back and tell him that Eli Jewett had been a good man, and the only one to kiss him on the forehead. "I'll bring supper down. I'm just up the hill, you know. There's no one closer."

She meant a kindness, but Cooper's face stiffened, and Mrs. Perley saw it. She left him alone to mourn more loudly than any top step could mourn.

And he did.

Alone. Upstairs in his room.

Clutched by the stillness of the house.

Until day was almost done, and the dark yellows of the sky passed through the lace curtains.

He heard Mrs. Perley come in and the screen door slam shut behind her. Almost immediately the smell of a croutoned casserole came up to him. He realized he was hungry, terribly hungry. He couldn't remember if he had partaken of any of the sandwiches.

He heard Mrs. Perley go to the front door again. Probably to pick up something she'd left on the porch. He didn't hear the screen door slam shut behind her. He sat up on his bed. She must be holding it open. Cooper waited. The door didn't close.

He grabbed a new shirt—he had wiped his face more than a couple of times with the sleeves of the one he had on—and walked to the upstairs hall window.

Looking out, he saw a black sedan, the dust of the road rising up behind it. It did not hurry.

When Cooper got downstairs, Mrs. Perley was still standing by the open screen door, staring outside.

"Mrs. Perley?" he said.

She turned to him as though startled. Then she grabbed him and held him to her. "Oh, Cooper," she said. She wrapped her arms around him tightly.

★ ★ ★ ★ ★ ★ ★ ★ ★

# CHAPTER TWO

WHEN COOPER WOKE, there was a moment when he didn't have to remember. He heard the familiar sounds of breakfast downstairs and smelled coffee again. Coffee! The radio was on low. The refrigerator door opened and closed, the faucet in the sink turned on and off.

He could almost believe it was his grandmother downstairs.

And then he remembered.

His grandmother was gone.

His grandfather was gone.

And he remembered Mrs. Perley holding him close against her, as though he were about to be swept away.

"What is it?" he had asked.

"Oh, Cooper," she said again. And then, "Come eat before it gets cold."

Cooper figured Mrs. Perley's solution to all the ills of the world was "come eat before it gets cold."

So they had—it was a chicken casserole with brussels sprouts, which no human being should have to eat, but he did to be polite. He tried once more to ask about the sedan, but when he did, she went out to bring in dessert, and who can ask questions over a lemon meringue?

This morning, she was at it again.

Cooper dressed, put on his grandfather's watch, and came downstairs. The dining room table was set for breakfast—golly Moses, the dining room table for breakfast—but Mrs. Perley shoved him through the kitchen and out toward the barn. "Morning milking first," she said, and Cooper nodded. Morning milking before everything else.

He didn't mind. He yawned once, stretched, and then stepped out into the dewy morning, the way he came out every morning now—alone.

When he got to the Big Barn, the doors were already open and the cows mooing in the too-bright electric light as Mr. Searle milked. "About time you were up," he said. "New Hampshire dairyman never sleeps in."

"Grandpa never uses the lights for morning milking. Just the lantern in winter."

"That so?"

"He says the cows milk better when they're still sleepy."

"Don't care to milk in the dark," said Mr. Searle. "Never did, never will. Be sure of that." He pointed. "Those on this side are done. You start on the other."

Cooper wanted to say that the barn was his barn, not Mr. Searle's. He wanted to say that milking by the dim light of morning was his favorite time of day. But he didn't. He started on the other side, not sure if he should be glad of the help or angry.

Angry, he decided. Definitely angry.

*Be sure of that,* he thought, and glared at Mr. Searle's back.

But it's hard to stay angry while leaning against the flank of a cow. Cooper liked milking. He liked the work of the hoses and the swish of the thick blue-white milk coming through them. Most especially, he liked tending Moon and Star, who didn't care to be milked by machine, thank you.

"It'll take forever if you milk by hand," said Mr. Searle, coming up behind him.

"Just these two. Moon and Star don't like it any other way."

"They'll have to get used to it, won't they?"

Cooper looked up at him. "I can stay up with the milking," he said.

"What are you, barely fifteen or so?"

"Or so."

Mr. Searle eyed him a moment. "Make sure you get

★ 23 ★

those pails to the cooler quick," he said, "and muck out proper." Then he left for his own place.

Cooper leaned against Moon and closed his eyes. He rubbed his forehead against her soft flank, then gathered the pails and carried them to the cooler.

He looked at his grandfather's watch; already he was late, even with Mr. Searle's help. He stacked hay bales by the stalls. He mucked out, not quite proper. Then he herded the cows out to the Far Pasture and came back to unload the grain sacks from Old Ford. He carried them one by one into the barn bins and wondered, if he really did look fifteen, whether Sheriff Gibbs might not fuss at him if he drove the pickup into town. He did well enough driving it around the farm, and except for the one apple tree that had jumped right out at him when it should have stayed put and the row of small cedars that his grandfather shouldn't have planted anyway and the mailbox that was too close to the driveway for anyone to turn around without hitting, he hadn't had much trouble at all.

With each sack, he thought of the last trip into New Lincoln with his grandfather, stopping to get groceries—where, Cooper suddenly remembered, he had seen a black sedan—and stopping at the feed and grain store—where the black sedan had been parked across the street.

And he thought of how they had left town early, even

though there had been some bolts to pick up at Hurd's Hardware, and even though they'd talked about staying late that day for the fresh triple-berry pies at the New Lincoln Diner.

And he thought of how his grandfather had watched the rearview mirror most of the way home and had clipped the mailbox as they turned into the driveway. "It's not like you haven't done it yourself," he had said to Cooper. Which was true.

Still, it was strange to miss a fresh triple-berry pie from the New Lincoln Diner.

When Cooper finished unloading the grain and came back through the barn, he glanced at the switch box. The current wasn't on to the electric fence around the Far Pasture. He threw the switch off, then back on again. Nothing. He shook his head. Grandpa would have fussed at him for not checking it before he brought the cows out.

He turned the switch to *Off* and went out to walk the fence. He walked all the way around the Far Pasture while the cows chewed slowly, their lovely brown eyes winking at him as he counted to be sure none had gotten out. Every step he took was one he had taken beside his grandfather. Every post they had dug together; every wire they had strung together.

He missed him like he would miss the sun if it fell out of the sky.

He came all the way around and finally found the break right behind the Big Barn. The post had been pushed in and both lines snapped clean. Funny thing: If a cow had leaned against the fence, she would have pushed it out. Something was more interested in getting in than getting out.

Cooper pushed the post back and stomped the dirt around it. He twisted the wires together—that would do for now—and then went back into the barn, checked the current, and closed the barn door.

He looked at his grandfather's watch again. Then he went in for breakfast at the dining room table.

He got to New Lincoln High late. Mrs. Perley wouldn't hear of him driving Old Ford into town, so she drove him herself—at about race pace. At school, no one talked to him much. He ate lunch alone until Peter Hurd sat next to him. They didn't talk much either. Through Geometry he thought about filling the grain bins from the sacks he had carried in that morning. And after he got home from freshman cross, there would be the Orchard to mow. And there was still some splitting for this winter's woodpile—he was behind on that—and more hay to haul to the barn loft. And that top porch step to fix.

He thought about the chores through every class and wondered how much he was missing what his grandfather used to do without saying anything about it. It worried him through World Cultures, where he found it hard to care much about Ancient Egyptian Trade Routes. And it worried him through English, where he couldn't muster up much concern for whether Beatrice served God, loved Benedick, and mended or not. But the ending of the play, when the prince was left all alone–that had something to it. He knew what that was about.

After school, he ran. The good thing about cross practice was that you couldn't think about anything except for running. But he hadn't run in five days, and though he ran his guts out, he wasn't even close to Peter by the end of the sixth mile. By the ninth mile, it was like he was in another race. He ended in a sweaty stupor, unable to think of anything but his next breath.

Which was just what he wanted.

He rode home on Peter's handlebars, Peter pedaling all the way to Cooper's driveway, which Reverend Hurd was just pulling out of.

"I only stopped for a moment," he called out, and drove away. Cooper jumped from the handlebars, and Peter took off after his father, racing behind the car to see who could get home first. Standing at the end of his drive, Cooper tried not to cry as he watched them.

He dropped his backpack on the front porch and went around to the Big Barn. All the grain bins had been filled, and most of the hay hauled up to the loft. Even the stalls had been mucked out proper. He tried to imagine Reverend Hurd gathering the bales under his Methodist arm and hauling them up the ladder. He tried to imagine him mucking out. And again, he tried not to cry.

He checked the gas and oil on the Farmall, then backed it out from under the shed, feeling the familiar rumbling and grumbling of the shaft beneath him. He drove around the Big Barn, bouncing with the hubbub of the machine, and set to mow the Orchard—well, half the Orchard. By then Mr. Searle was up and there was evening milking to do. He let the wood splitting go, since after milking there was mucking out proper again. But he did finish hauling up the rest of the hay.

If Mrs. Perley hadn't made him sit for supper—at the dining room table again!—he would have come back in from the barn and fallen asleep without eating a thing. As it was, he barely ate what was left of the casserole. Though he did well enough with the lemon meringue pie.

As for homework: If Mrs. Perley hadn't brought his backpack in from the front porch, he would have forgotten he'd left it there. Not that it would have made much difference. He went up to his room with it but never opened it that night. Geometry theorems went unproved, Ancient Egyptian Trade Routes went unmapped, and Benedick's blank verse went unscanned.

Cooper slept without moving all night long.

And when he woke up in the morning, there wasn't even a moment when he didn't remember that he had to do it ALL OVER AGAIN.

That's how it went for three days. Cooper tried to keep up. Mrs. Perley brought down supper. She stayed overnight while Cooper slept without moving. And in the morning, she made breakfast and set it out on the dining room table while Cooper milked with Mr. Searle.

By the end of the third day, Cooper knew he couldn't keep up. His teachers were used to him not doing homework, but not him sleeping through Geometry, World Cultures, English—and golly Moses, PE, for crying out loud. He figured that the good Lord simply hadn't stuffed enough hours in the day for him to finish the chores that had to get finished—even with Mr. Searle and Mrs. Perley helping.

And his running was terrible. He knew Coach was holding back from saying what he wanted to say only because he was a kid with no dog, no brothers or sisters, no parents, and no grandparents. And he could see it wasn't easy for him to hold back. "You're coming along, Cooper," he would say, his voice choked. "Coming along."

So one afternoon, home after cross practice, Cooper put off mowing and went into the parlor. He ran his fingers along the top of his grandmother's rocker and then opened his grandfather's desk. The sweet tobacco smell of him came up out of the drawers, and Cooper stopped for a moment to breathe it in like memory. Then he started looking through the folders—Grange reports, milk schedules, equipment manuals, USDA recommendations—even a folder of annual reports for the New Lincoln Methodist Church. He looked for any folder with the name of some Jewett somewhere, anywhere.

And he found one: a folder marked, simply, *Cooper Jewett.*

It held a birth certificate for him from Keene Memorial Hospital, with his last name inked out and with his parents' names inked out.

It held a medical report for him, with a footprint, a handprint, and a note that he was born at eight pounds, two and a quarter ounces, at 8:35 on the evening of his birthday, with a list of immunizations and possible allergies—and his last name inked out.

And it had an envelope addressed to Eli and Edna Jewett, New Lincoln, New Hampshire, but with no letter.

That was all. His whole life in a folder marked *Cooper Jewett.* With half of his name inked out. And an empty envelope.

He said his name aloud: "Cooper Jewett." Then he shuffled the papers back together and closed the folder. Weighing it in his hand, he carried it upstairs and slid it underneath his mattress. Then he went out to mow the other half of the Orchard. He ate supper that night without any failed silence.

"You all right, Cooper?" Mrs. Perley asked.

He nodded.

That night he lay in his bed, his arms behind his head. He said his name out loud in the dark that moved slowly around him. "Cooper Jewett."

For the first time in his life, he wondered what it meant.

In the morning he woke early, even before Mrs. Perley was up and moving around the kitchen. It was not yet dawn and the sky was still mostly purple, but he was suddenly wide awake. He stretched and wondered what had woken him up. Then he knew. He'd heard a moo where there shouldn't have been a moo. He looked out the window over his bed and saw six of the cows—not Moon and Star, who were good and true—trampling the carrots in his grandmother's vegetable garden.

He ran down, still in his pajamas. First things first: Cooper opened the gate to the Near Pasture and then ran behind the cows, waving and hallooing to herd them in. Then he checked the fence, and he was right about where to begin. The same post had been pushed in again, and the wires that Cooper had twisted together were broken cleanly, as if with a cutter.

Which is exactly what he found on the barn floor when he went in to shut off the power. He picked it up and held it. "Dang," he said—which was about as close to a cuss as his grandfather would have ever let him say, even in the barn. It wasn't enough that he could barely keep up. Someone was out to make it even harder.

When Mr. Searle came up to the barn that morning, Cooper looked at him with suspicious eyes. "You ever seen this?" he asked, holding up the wire cutter.

"Wire cutter," said Mr. Searle. He took it from Cooper. "Pretty good wire cutter." He handed it back. "Nope, never did see it before."

Cooper wasn't sure he believed him.

Through milking, Cooper was madder than all get-out. Golly Moses, to cut a man's wires!

Through breakfast he fumed, and he almost snapped at Mrs. Perley when she asked him to pass the brown sugar. "Gracious goodness," she said under her breath.

And so maybe it could be expected that Cooper would be tempted to use words that his grandfather didn't ever allow when he got his bike out to head toward school and saw a black sedan idling at the end of his driveway. Cooper put up his hand to shadow his eyes against the rising sun. Two Very Big Men stood outside the car, one taking pictures. The other pointed at him.

"Hey," yelled Cooper.

The man with the camera took another picture.

"Who do you think you are?" Cooper hollered.

They both jumped into the car and sped away.

That's when Cooper used the words.

Cooper rode to school in the distant wake of the black sedan, trailing anger like a long shroud behind him. He watched for the sedan as he coasted down to the Hurds' house, then pedaled back up onto the pavement of Main Street, turned on Whittier, and so came to New Lincoln High School.

And that's when he saw it. Actually, that's when he saw four black sedans—all idling quietly, tense, a pride with their tinted windows drawn up and impassable.

His anger froze, and Cooper shivered. He rode by slowly, hardly pedaling. Most everyone who rode by, rode by slowly.

Peter was waiting for him on the steps.

"So, Jewett, you want to know what *four* cars like that are doing in New Lincoln?"

"You counted them all by yourself. You must be in advanced math."

"Shut up, Jewett. You want to know as much as I do."

*More,* thought Cooper.

But they both found out during homeroom announcements, when Ms. Dove declared that first-hour classes were canceled—cheers from the homerooms, relief from

Cooper who hadn't finished his Map of Ancient Egyptian Trade Routes yet—and that instead the students would Quietly and Promptly gather together in the Fine Arts Auditorium, where they would be afforded the great honor of being addressed by Senator Wickham, candidate for the Democratic nomination for President of the United States. Senator Wickham would speak to them about "Citizenship and the Young Person"—groans from the homerooms—and Ms. Dove was sure that they would each and all appreciate the opportunity to witness Democracy itself in action. Would classes please come as soon as attendance was taken?

Peter and Cooper let themselves be carried along in the tidal surge of the hallways. They flowed into the auditorium—"Quietly and Promptly!" Ms. Dove beckoned at the doors—and spread out into the seats, staring at the stage. For there he sat, his legs crossed, an easy smile on his face, his silver hair as perfect as it was on television. Senator Wickham himself. And Hannah Joyce with him, her smile all toothy.

When the waves finally settled—neither quietly nor promptly—Ms. Dove stood to introduce Hannah Joyce. "We are so fortunate to have a media celebrity with us as well this morning!" And then Hannah Joyce stood to introduce Senator Wickham.

Cooper heard none of this. He watched the Senator's eyes scanning the auditorium, settling on each face for a moment, touching it, scrutinizing it, and then moving on. Cooper saw the eyes moving down the rows, one by one, as Hannah Joyce spoke. Then she stepped back and the Senator stood. He buttoned his jacket. Words began to come out of his mouth, but his smile did not change. His eyes continued down the rows. One by one.

Then down Cooper's row.

Cooper felt the eyes coming, and he shrank back against his seat. His hands gripped his knees tightly. The eyes came closer, and Cooper hunched down. Peter looked at him. "Is something wrong with you?" Then Cooper saw the eyes slip over Peter's face. They came onto his own.

And stopped.

The words kept coming, the smile did not change.

But Senator Wickham's eyes did not leave Cooper's face for one minute, two minutes, four minutes. And though the words he spoke were of citizenship and the responsibility of our nation's young people and the agenda of the America for Wickham campaign, his eyes said to Cooper, "I know you."

★ ★ ★ ★ ★ ★ ★ ★ ★

# CHAPTER THREE

Senator Wickham's address lasted only a half hour, so Cooper wasn't saved after all. He went on to World Cultures and had to admit to Mr. Hupfer that the Ancient Egyptian Trade Routes were still uncharted. Peter tried not to look like a traitor as he handed in his own map.

Cooper shrugged. It wasn't that big a deal. It was just a map. The ancient Egyptians were all dead. They'd get along without it.

But when he got to PE the next hour and Coach stopped him by his locker and told him to report to Ms. Dove's office, he wondered if it might be a bigger deal than he thought. Golly Moses, reporting to the principal's office over the Ancient Egyptian Trade Routes!

But it wasn't over the trade routes.

Ms. Dove's secretary stared at him when he came in. She pointed to Ms. Dove's door, which opened even before he had a chance to knock. "Cooper," Ms. Dove said, "there's someone who has heard about you and wants to meet you." She took his arm and brought him inside. "Senator Wickham, this is Cooper Jewett."

Senator Wickham was sitting behind Ms. Dove's desk, beside a Very Big Man who stood mountainously still. The Senator stood up slowly. "It's good to meet you, Cooper," he said, and held out his hand.

Cooper remembered what his grandfather had said Senator Wickham's hands held. But what could he do? He reached out and took hold. He'd wash his hands later.

Senator Wickham turned to the Very Big Man. "New Hampshire's schools have a great many needs these days. Perhaps Ms. Dove might be willing to tour you around," he said. He turned to her. "After next November, there will be an administration in Washington eager to help out with our school systems. The more we know, the better."

He laughed politely, and Ms. Dove laughed with him. "Certainly," she said. "And it will give you a chance to talk with Cooper."

"Thank you," said Senator Wickham. The Very Big Man followed Ms. Dove out of her office.

Cooper felt abandoned. And again he felt the Senator's eyes settle on his face.

"You know who I am." Senator Wickham wasn't asking.

Cooper nodded. Everyone in New Hampshire knew who he was.

"It won't be long before you'll be able to tell all your friends at school that you stood this close to a President of the United States."

Cooper nodded again.

"You going to vote for me?"

Cooper considered how he should answer. "My grandfather says you should vote for someone you can be sure about," he said finally.

"I'll take that as a yes. Your grandfather was a plainspoken and honest man, and he told you the truth. I'd like to have met him."

"He died a few days ago."

"I know," said Senator Wickham.

Cooper looked hard at him.

"When I become President, Cooper, I want to be the kind of man your grandfather talked about—someone you can be sure about. And if I'm going to be that kind of President, I'll have to know what's going on not only in Washington, D.C., but in New Lincoln, New Hampshire, too."

Senator Wickham picked up a folder from the desk

and held it as his eyes came back to Cooper. "Have you been following the campaign?"

"Things could be better, couldn't they?" Cooper couldn't stop himself. It was exactly what his grandfather would have said.

Senator Wickham smiled. "I suppose. But things have a way of turning around. Sooner than you might imagine."

"I suppose," said Cooper.

"That's actually one reason I'm here today. That, and meeting you. I'm looking for help to turn it around." He held the folder to his chest. "Will you help me with that, son?"

"Mr. Wickham—"

"*Senator* Wickham."

"Senator Wickham, what could I do?"

"You could want to make a difference. That's how it starts, Cooper. Wanting to make a difference."

But Cooper wasn't sure that he wanted to make a difference for Senator Wickham. And as things were, he was barely keeping up. He shook his head. "I've got this whole dairy farm to take care of. And a trade map due in World Cultures. And Coach is about to kick me off freshman cross if my running doesn't pick up. Golly Moses, even if there was something I could do, I couldn't fit in a single thing more. Not and go to sleep before it's time to get up."

"I know that 'making a difference' sounds like a cliché, Cooper. Almost everything I said today in your auditorium was a cliché. Being a good citizen. Taking responsibility. Voting your conscience. All clichés. But being a cliché doesn't make something not true. And being a cliché doesn't mean it can't be good, honorable, and important work for your country."

"I suppose."

"You suppose right." Senator Wickham came around from behind the desk. He sat on its edge. "You're a bright young boy. Come on the campaign trail with me. You could represent the needs of all the farmers in New Hampshire. In America! A kid who will stand up even if it means standing up all by himself." He raised his hand as though he were typing out bold headlines in the air: "AMERICA'S FARMERS MUST NEVER BE ABANDONED. Something like that."

And the thrill washed over Cooper. The campaign trail! Traveling across America with someone with steel hair and glinty eyes who might be the next President of the United States! Going to cities he'd heard about only on television. Maybe getting interviewed by Hannah Joyce. Flying in planes!

Golly Moses!

But then who would milk Moon and Star by hand?

Cooper heard their soft mooing, felt their warm flanks against his cheeks.

Senator Wickham walked over to Ms. Dove's window and looked out. "You live on a dairy farm of, what, fifty cows?"

"Sixty-four cows."

"Sixty-four cows. Do you know how many dairy farms in New Hampshire with under three hundred cows are making a profit, Cooper? The low percentage would surprise you. But here's what is amazing: They don't give up. Just like you. They don't give up. And because they don't give up, they make a difference."

"I can't give up."

"No, I guess you can't." Senator Wickham turned around. "And you can help others not give up." He went back to Ms. Dove's desk and spread out what was in the folder. "Come look." Cooper went up to the desk. He had spread out glossy pictures. Pictures of Cooper. Pictures of him milking. Mucking out. Stroking Moon. Stroking Star. Carrying pails of milk out to the cooler. Hauling bales up the ladder.

Cooper felt himself stiffen—quietly and promptly.

"I know it's a surprise. We had cameras put in your barn so we could get real-life photos. It's always obvious when they're posed."

Cooper was glad he hadn't been picking his nose. "For what?" he asked.

"For the difference, Cooper."

And Cooper felt the thrill again. Like little carbonated

bubbles rushing all through his bloodstream after an Admiral Ames Root Beer.

"What about school?"

"I've already talked to Ms. Dove about that. She agrees that the education you'd get in a year of travel across the country with the America for Wickham campaign would beat a year studying world cultures in textbooks."

Of course she'd agree, thought Cooper. Having a student from New Lincoln High on the campaign trail would put the school in headlines most every day in New Hampshire. But maybe it wouldn't be so bad, he thought. He could leave off trying to keep up.

*You're my first boy, Cooper, my first boy.*

Cooper heard his grandfather's voice as plainly as if his grandfather were there, tousling his hair. He almost was able to feel his hand. He could almost smell him— he was that close.

"I can't go, Senator Wickham," he said. "There's the cows. There's the whole farm."

Senator Wickham did not look pleased. "No, Cooper, there isn't. Eli Jewett's farm is in debt up to its fence posts. To a"—he looked in the folder—"Farnham Searle. He couldn't make it pay, and you can't make it pay. There's no telling when it will be taken away from you. And even if it was free and clear, which it isn't, the state won't let you live there for long. Not by yourself. If you truly want to make a difference, you'll come with me. We could do some fine things, Cooper. Maybe turn this campaign around."

Cooper felt little carbonated bubbles busting in his heart.

In debt up to its fence posts? Taken away? Farnham Searle? Mr. Searle?

"You never know how just one small thing could win or lose an election," said Senator Wickham. He took a photo from the desk and held it up. "A thing like a picture of a young, determined American boy, struggling to keep his farm going against all odds, alone, with no help from a White House that couldn't care less about the small American farmer."

Cooper looked at the photo of himself, and suddenly he thought of cameras, clipped wires, pushed-in posts.

"And, Cooper, come next year, how would you like to be welcome at the White House?"

There were cows in his grandmother's garden, Cooper thought. All for some pictures that he didn't ask for.

"The Blue Room," said Senator Wickham. "The Roosevelt Room. The Lincoln Bedroom. The Oval Office. You'd be welcome in them all, Cooper, as the Boy Who Helped Win the Election. What's a played-out New Hampshire farm to that?"

And right then, Cooper knew what he wanted. Maybe

he didn't have a dog or a brother or sister or mother or father or even grandparents anymore. But he did have a dairy farm. And maybe it was played out. And maybe Mr. Farnham Searle did own it up to its fence posts. Still, there wasn't any part of it that wasn't a part of him—even a top porch step that groaned.

"I'm sorry, Senator Wickham. I can't leave."

There was a light knock. "Senator Wickham?" called Ms. Dove through the door.

Senator Wickham looked at his watch. "Son, you are exasperating. I've negotiated international trade treaties that were easier than this. You listen: You'll leave with me and head out on the campaign trail and become the most famous farm boy in America, or you'll leave with New Hampshire Social Services in a day or two and head out to an institution with high walls and dormitories with metal beds. The state will sell off your cows and take down the barns and auction off the land to some developer who'll put up a shopping mall and upscale condominiums for people from Boston who imagine they want to live the country life. You won't be able to say moo before it's all gone. That's the choice. So after school, you go on home and pack a suitcase. Gather up any documents that show who you are—birth certificate, medical records, papers like those."

"Senator—"

"I'm offering you the chance of a lifetime, Cooper. Don't make me regret I had to pressure you into it. Whole countries have regretted making me wait."

And that was when Cooper heard Ms. Dove cry, "Just a moment, please." The door flung open, and there was Mrs. Perley, standing with Ms. Dove at her back. With her hands on her hips, Mrs. Perley looked like a force of nature.

Senator Wickham crossed the room and held out his hand. "Mrs. Perley, I'm guessing."

She looked at his hand, and Cooper knew what she was thinking. But what could she do? She reached out and took hold.

"Lately retired from New Lincoln Elementary."

"Yes," she said.

"Where you taught for over thirty years while serving on boards and commissions at both county and state levels with distinction and directing school plays and musicals on occasion."

"I was a wonder," said Mrs. Perley. "I even had charge of the bathroom key for both fifth-grade classrooms. Imagine that."

"And the widow of the much-decorated Captain Perley."

"Yes, I am."

"And much decorated yourself."

"You know too much about my life, Senator."

"Never too much," he said, and finally let go of her hand. "Cooper and I were discussing something of a partnership, Mrs. Perley. I'll let him tell you about it and perhaps you might persuade him."

"I've found over the years that Cooper Jewett could, like his grandparents, stand on his own two feet."

"It's not a question of whether he's standing, Mrs. Perley." Senator Wickham looked at Cooper. "It's a question of where he'll be standing."

"He will be standing right here in New Lincoln," she said. Cooper felt the little carbonated bubbles in his bloodstream dissolving.

"Well," said Senator Wickham, smiling as if for the cameras, "think about my offer, Cooper. The farmers of New Hampshire are depending on you. The farmers of America are depending on you to make a difference." And he left the office, still smiling. Ms. Dove followed.

Mrs. Perley rubbed her hand against her jacket. "He is one of those of whom you can never be sure," she said.

"Don't worry, Mrs. Perley. I wouldn't vote for him even if I could."

"I should certainly hope not."

"I'll be too busy standing right here in New Lincoln."

"Yes, you will," she said, and put her arm around his shoulders and held him tightly.

"How did you know where I was?"

She held him at arm's length and looked at him, shocked. "I was an elementary school teacher," she said. "I know everything. Let's go wash our hands."

By third hour, it was all over New Lincoln High that Senator Wickham had met Cooper in Ms. Dove's office—and for a long time. It was also all over New Lincoln High that Cooper had met with Senator Wickham because his parents had been involved in espionage activity and the FBI wanted to know everything that Cooper knew. And because the President had heard his story and was setting up a federal trust for him worth a cool million dollars. And because Cooper was going to go to Washington, D.C., to work for the Department of Agriculture.

Peter didn't see him again until English. "So what did Wickham really say?"

"He asked me to be part of his campaign and travel around with him for a year."

"Jewett, don't be such a jerk. What did he really want?"

"That's what he wanted."

Peter shook his head. "All right. If you don't want to tell me—"

"Okay," said Cooper. "Okay. He heard that I could drive Ford pickups and wanted to know if I would like to drive one of his sedans around the school."

"Really?"

"Really. But when I asked him if it had a stick, he said it didn't. I said I've never driven anything without a stick, so I'd better not try his sedan first off. And then he said okay. And that's it."

"So you didn't try it."

"No."

"There's something wrong with you," said Peter.

The next day was Saturday, and Cooper missed the freshman cross meet. He didn't even think of it until it was too late to make the bus. And Mrs. Perley had asked Mr. Searle to come up to breakfast after morning milking, so he couldn't ask her to drive him over to Keene for the meet. He couldn't bear to have Mr. Searle snort at him again, like he was only a kid who couldn't keep up. So he spent the morning splitting and stacking winter's wood, and after lunch he drew his dang Map of Ancient Egyptian Trade Routes. After supper he harvested the carrots that hadn't been eaten or trampled, and then he raked over the ruts the cows had left to make his grandmother's garden look presentable.

He faced the road while he worked. He watched for black sedans.

He kept up that day, but whatever it was that had stopped in him when his grandfather had died still hung broken. He felt it deep, like a stone too big to heft out of the garden. He just had to hoe around it and make do.

The next day, Mrs. Perley drove off early to the Church of St. Perpetua. She offered to take Cooper, but his grandparents had thought Mass was awfully Catholic, something a proper Methodist should not get involved in.

It was only after she'd left and he'd cleaned up in the kitchen that he looked at his grandfather's watch and thought maybe he should head over to church. And soon afterward, he was driving Old Ford to New Lincoln Methodist, and not a single apple tree, cedar, or mailbox got in the way. No one who saw him drive past could have missed him—the muffler on the pickup had rusted through about a hundred years ago—but they might not have guessed that he was sitting on top of his grandfather's tractor cushion and that every time he reached down for the clutch, he began to sweat. There was the bad moment when Sheriff Gibbs drove slowly by him, but Cooper kept his eyes ahead, lifted two fingers off the wheel to give a wave, and drove on.

He kept below the speed limit and parked on the far side of New Lincoln Common.

The transactions at the church were pretty much as they always were, and though Cooper felt strange sitting in his pew with an empty spot next to him, it was good to hear Mrs. Hurd playing the familiar hymns too slowly, to see the choir in maroon robes now faded to a kind of sour pink, to sit behind the great tribe of Hurds taking up the front two pews, and even to listen to Reverend Hurd's sermon on—well, Cooper never could quite remember what his sermons were about.

Then after the services, Mrs. Hurd gathered him up as she swept past, and he found himself one of the crowd at the Hurd home, sitting down between Peter and John to a Sunday pancake lunch, with two gallons of milk on the table, a quart of maple syrup, a couple of pounds of butter, three—no, four—dozen sausages, and enough pancakes to feed a logging camp, none of which were left on the table when things were done.

And until things were done, Meg Hurd had to talk about her new yellow dress with daffodils on it even though it wasn't springtime, and David Hurd had to talk about Jimmy Hupfer, who stuck a marble up his nose in the church nursery, and how his favorite marble was now covered with—"Never mind," said Mrs. Hurd—and Rebecca Hurd had to talk about whether she could please please please please go see this new movie that every other kid in her class was seeing and that only had a little violence and—"Never mind," said Mrs. Hurd; "Not on God's green earth," said Reverend Hurd—and Ben Hurd and James Hurd had to see who could eat the most pancakes without throwing up, and Kathleen Hurd had to talk about the new cook in the New Lincoln

Diner who had tattoos on his arms and someone said on his—"Never mind," said Reverend and Mrs. Hurd at the same time. And all this came at once, stuck in between bites, so that Cooper couldn't decide if it was like a carnival or like Armageddon.

Whatever it was, it wasn't lonely.

Cooper drove home slowly after lunch—very slowly, since Reverend Hurd insisted on driving behind him. (He knew Cooper was only fourteen.) Eight of the Hurds had asked if they could ride in the back of Old Ford, and Mrs. Hurd said that they could . . .

*if* Cooper drove very slowly,
*if* Peter rode in the back to keep everyone still,
*if* they didn't horse around,
*if* they all kept their hands inside,
and *if*—

"Good Lord, it's just over the hill," said Reverend Hurd.

"That doesn't make it safe," said Mrs. Hurd.

But Cooper made it back without carnage and even negotiated the turn into the driveway without clipping the mailbox. Then the Hurds stuffed themselves in the station wagon and waved good-bye, and Cooper went into a house as empty as an envelope without a letter. He slept the rest of the afternoon on the parlor couch and woke up when he started to get cold. It wouldn't be long before he'd have to keep the woodstove up. He ate a liverwurst and onion sandwich that Mrs. Perley had left for him—which tasted a lot better than it sounded—and three raspberry tarts. Then calling the cows in from the Far Pasture, evening milking, and mucking out. Mrs. Perley was back by then, and she asked Mr. Searle to stay over for supper, which he did. They ate in the dining room again.

Some Geometry, some scanning of Benedick's lines, some last changes to the trade routes. And so they came to the end of the day. Mrs. Perley went on in to bed, but Cooper stayed in the parlor, slumped onto the couch, and turned on the late news: There was Hannah Joyce again, reporting on the primary debate between the President and Senator Wickham. How his grandfather would have loved to hear this.

The President was all about farm subsidies—Cooper figured he would have to learn something about those. They sounded like good news for wiry, cantankerous New Hampshire dairymen. In fact, the President promised a whole pile of promises to New Hampshire. At least, it seemed so. Senator Wickham was all about family values and the current administration's lack of respect for the small farmer. He promised a whole lot too. They fussed at each other back and forth, Senator Wickham's nose flaring, the President's green eyes glaring, until Cooper turned them both off. "That'll do for them tonight," he said.

He turned out the parlor lights, then the ones in the hall. In the kitchen he left one on in case he needed something with sugar in the middle of the night. Then he headed upstairs and, at the top, paused to look out the window over the farm.

An orange glow flickered across the front yard and spread up into the sky. He had never seen anything like it before. He wondered if that was what the northern lights were. Sometimes the light grew bright and jumped up high. And sometimes it grew even brighter, almost yellow, almost white.

Then he smelled smoke.

He opened the window, craning himself around as if he might see past the corner of the house.

But he didn't need to see—he knew already.

The Small Barn was on fire.

# CHAPTER FOUR

By the time Cooper reached his front porch, most of the Small Barn was shrouded in flames.

By the time he was halfway across the yard, he could hear Mrs. Perley calling, "Gracious goodness, Cooper, stay away from that fire."

And by the time he reached the Small Barn, he could make out Mr. Searle ducking in and out, sparks flitting around him like fireflies, hauling out milk cans and harnesses as fast as he could.

"This barn's gone," he yelled at Cooper. "Get a hose on the Big Barn before it catches too."

Cooper stared at the eager flames.

"Now!" yelled Mr. Searle. "Big Barn goes up, we might not get all the cows out."

Then Mrs. Perley was there. Cooper turned the water

on, and while Mrs. Perley took the hose and sprayed the side of the Big Barn closest to the fire, he ran inside to yank the frightened cows from their stalls. Every time he came out to lead one to the Near Pasture, the heat of the glow struck him like a fist.

Soon the flames of the Small Barn flared too hot for Mr. Searle, and he went to tug out the cows with Cooper—which was a help since they weren't coming out of their stalls with anything like eagerness. Their eyes were wide, and their feet splayed.

"Stick your fingers up their noses," hollered Mr. Searle.

Cooper looked at him. "In their snot?"

"Like this," said Mr. Searle, and he plunged his two fingers in and began to pull. The cow, of course, followed.

So Cooper and Mr. Searle pulled all the cows out of the Big Barn—except for Moon and Star, who followed when Cooper called them. And as he pulled them out, Cooper looked across the yard and watched the boards of the Small Barn fall away one by one in a great clattering of sparks. Then the blue fire leaped along the beams, until they too fell and spattered up more sparks than there were stars in the sky.

Cooper thought he might throw up.

Afterward, the three of them stood by the glowing ruin. "I'll run inside to call the sheriff," said Mr. Searle. "Not that he'll be awake this late." He went on in, while the cows mooed unhappily at the strange smell of smoke and being out in the pasture this late at night. The embers sizzled as the water from the hose Mrs. Perley still held steamed onto them.

"Thank goodness it was not the Big Barn," said Mrs. Perley.

They stood together in silence that worked until Mr. Searle came back.

"No answer. Not that I expected any," said Mr. Searle. "Darnedest thing I ever did see. Two hundred years these buildings stand, then Eli Jewett passes on, and the barn goes up quick as a firecracker. Darnedest thing I ever did see." He looked at Cooper. "Seems like someone's trying to tell you something."

He took the hose from Mrs. Perley and held it toward the heat of the ruin. "I'll finish up here," said Mr. Searle, "then head on home." He turned to Cooper. "Farm's no place for a boy alone. Maybe you'll see that now."

Cooper looked evenly at Mr. Searle. "How'd you see the fire so quickly?" he asked.

"Last thing a farmer does before he goes to bed is to check his own place. Doesn't hurt to look over to his neighbors'. Besides, a real farmer knows in his bones when something's wrong."

Mr. Searle faced into the heat. And Cooper, watching him silhouetted against the glow, still wondered how it was that he had seen the fire so quickly.

Mrs. Perley put her arm around Cooper's shoulders. "We will see to everything in the morning," she said, and he let her bring him to the house. She made up some hot milk—Cooper hated hot milk—and walked with him to the bottom of the stairs. "Get some sleep now," she said. "There is nothing more to do until morning."

And that was when Cooper saw the scattered papers that had meandered into the downstairs hallway. He went into the parlor, followed by Mrs. Perley, and felt himself walking over paper.

Then he switched on the light by his grandfather's desk.

And they gasped. "Gracious goodness," said Mrs. Perley.

There wasn't a single book on the shelves that hadn't been thrown down. There wasn't a single drawer from the desk that hadn't been taken out and dumped. The couch was overturned. The pictures were thrown from the walls. And it was all as muddled and jumbled together as if the tempest of the flames had whirled in and scattered it all to kingdom come.

"Mrs. Perley, maybe you'd better call Sheriff Gibbs again," said Cooper. Mrs. Perley nodded.

She let the phone ring for a long time, and when Sheriff Gibbs told her that, dang it, she had woken him up from an early bedtime, she said that she did not care. It was Sunday night, he said, and he was off duty, and it was late. Whatever it was, surely it could wait until morning.

"No," Mrs. Perley said, and Cooper could imagine her voice in a fifth-grade classroom. "It can most certainly not wait until morning. Come immediately." Then she hung up.

Cooper wasn't sure that Sheriff Gibbs would come, but he did, having driven slowly. He got out of his patrol car slowly, came onto the steps slowly, and stood rubbing his chin—of which there was a considerable amount to rub—while Mrs. Perley told him what had happened—a fire, a break-in, a room torn apart.

He wasn't all that helpful. "Mrs. Perley," he asked, "who'd want to break into Eli and Edna's?"

"Apparently someone had that desire."

"And why would they do that?"

"Those are the kinds of questions that police departments specialize in asking."

"Huh," said Sheriff Gibbs.

They went inside, the sheriff on ahead and holding out his flashlight. He shone it all around the wreck of the parlor—even though the light was on.

"Huh," he said again. He rubbed his chin. "What is it exactly that you want me to do?"

"Investigate!" said Mrs. Perley.

"Investigate a fire that likely as not started from an electrical problem? And a room that got messed up because someone was looking for something? Doesn't seem to me like a whole lot to investigate."

"There's no electric in the Small Barn," said Cooper.

"There," said Mrs. Perley.

"Huh," said Sheriff Gibbs.

"Sheriff Gibbs, the vocabulary of the English language is the wonder of the whole world. Chaucer spoke it and Shakespeare and Winston Churchill. With such a precedent, you could possibly make better use of it," said Mrs. Perley.

"Huh," said Sheriff Gibbs.

"Raymond Gibbs, I should have held you back when you were in fifth grade. I never have understood how this town elected you sheriff."

"Because Chaucer and Shakespeare and Winston Churchill weren't around to elect. Mrs. Perley, you should be figuring what to do with a boy alone on a farm. Maybe he reads Shakespeare every single night of his life, but he can't go on like this. He needs to go where someone can take care of him."

"I'm not leaving this farm," said Cooper.

"Well, do what you want. Pretty soon, it might not be up to you to decide anyway." He yawned, and his great chin fell like a load. "Nothing more to do here tonight. I'll be back up when I can to file a report. Meanwhile, you might as well leave all this alone. I suppose it'll be evidence."

"And that is your investigation," said Mrs. Perley.

"New Lincoln police, always at your service." He clicked his flashlight off and left. The top porch step shrieked when he touched it. Standing at the screen door, they watched him drive away in the patrol car. Slowly.

"What an unpleasant man," said Mrs. Perley. "I suppose that is what happens when we cease wanting to become our best selves."

"I'll make do, Mrs. Perley."

She put her arm around him and hugged him tightly. "Of course you will," she said, but even this far away, they both felt the heat of the Small Barn's embers.

Through the night, Cooper could see their glow in the air as he lay awake, missing his grandfather and his grandmother, wishing he could think of them without crying. But he couldn't.

The embers were still glowing the next morning when Cooper went out to bring the cows back into the Big Barn for milking. Mr. Searle was waiting for them. "Quiet this morning, boy."

"I guess I'm tired." He leaned his head against Star, and she brought herself around a bit to make him comfortable.

"It's five-thirty in the morning, best part of the day. How can you be tired for the best part of the day?"

"It does seem something of a miracle, doesn't it?"

"Boy, every dairy farmer has his ups and downs. So you've had a down. Maybe the property is worth a little bit less, but there's still the cows."

"Don't worry about the property being worth a little bit less."

"I'm not worried. You keeping up with everything?"

"Yes."

"Your schoolwork too?"

"Yes."

"Mrs. Perley's worried about you, you know."

"She doesn't need to be."

"The Methodist parson too."

"He doesn't need to be."

"That's what I told them. But they are anyway. Worried sick that there's no one to come for you and you sitting here all alone."

"Tell them I'll be all right."

Mr. Searle pointed his finger at Cooper. "Best thing for you would be if someone came to run this farm. And before it's worth a whole lot less."

Cooper looked at him. "I figure I can do it myself."

"You figure wrong."

It wasn't the best start to the week. And it didn't help that he got clobbered in World Cultures for forgetting to bring in his Map of Ancient Egyptian Trade Routes and that Mr. Hupfer clearly didn't believe him when he said it was done. And it really didn't help that

Coach made him run the bleachers three times in PE for missing Saturday's meet. And it really, really didn't help that Ms. Dove saw him in the hall and told him that she had most of the paperwork finished for his time away from school with the America for Wickham campaign.

Cooper felt the farm slipping from him. And with it, his grandmother and grandfather.

*You're my first boy, Cooper, my first boy.*

At supper that night, neither Cooper nor Mrs. Perley said a thing—Cooper because what was broken in him was as heavy as Grief, and Mrs. Perley because she had caught a terrible cold. "All that night air," she croaked. She patted her chest and didn't eat a single raspberry tart for dessert.

After supper, Cooper cleaned up while she sat in his grandmother's rocker. Then he went into his grandparents' room and found the horehounds. He brought out his grandmother's afghan and spread it around her shoulders. Then holding her arm, he walked her back up to her house—"You'll be a whole lot more comfortable in your own room," he said.

"I do not want to leave you all alone," she said.

"What could happen? I'll go home and fall asleep. Then I'll wake up and milk."

"The very first thing in the morning, I will be down," she said.

Cooper didn't argue. He watched her go upstairs and went into her kitchen to make a cup of tea in a dainty pink teacup. When he brought it up, she had already settled deeply under two quilts and was almost asleep. He left the tea steaming by her bedside. And he leaned over and kissed her lightly on the forehead.

Cooper went home and up to bed, but he did not fall asleep. He lay in the dark with his arms behind his head. He couldn't keep Mr. Searle's words from sounding in his ears. *You figure wrong. You figure wrong.* The night peepers called from the pond, and two or three times he heard the screech of a small animal—the owls were out. One of the cows was mooing in the barn, and the wind, trying to decide which direction to blow in, was creaking the weathervane around and around.

Finally he got out of bed and looked out the window. Nothing at the end of the driveway but the lights he had left on at Mrs. Perley's were still bright up the hill. Cooper was surprised at how warm they seemed. He glanced at his grandfather's watch. Well after midnight. It was too late to call Mrs. Perley to see if she was all right.

It wasn't too late to go down to the kitchen to see about another raspberry tart.

But when he threw the light switch in his room, nothing came on. He tried the light in the hallway. Nothing. He went downstairs. The light in the kitchen was off.

Cooper groped his way over to the kitchen telephone. When he picked it up, it was dead.

And then the top porch step groaned.

The dark went very quiet.

Cooper felt his heartbeat quicken.

The top porch step groaned again.

Cooper slid quietly back into the front hall, gliding his hand along the wall in the dark. He shivered, and not just because the night was promising a frost, and not just because he had on only his shorts. The porch step groaned again, and Cooper crouched low, peering around the stairway. Through the lace curtains in the front-door window, he could make out a Very Big Figure.

It was not Mrs. Perley.

He had no doubt he was from the black sedans.

Still crouching, Cooper scooted across the hallway and slid the door bolt to. Then he backed up to the kitchen and tried the telephone again. Dead as a door-nail. He put the receiver down quietly, then jerked against the sink as a slice of yellow light stabbed into the darkness of the kitchen, probing up and down. It slid along the woodstove, across into his grandmother's checked curtains, and past them until it struck the picture of his grandparents on the wall. His grandparents— who would not smile even when he photographed them for their fiftieth anniversary—glowered back.

Then the knob on the kitchen door turned, jiggling back and forth.

Cooper ducked beneath the table and held his knees to his chest.

The beam of light flicked off, and a pane of glass in the front door shattered.

The knob on the kitchen door turned and jiggled again.

Cooper huddled under the table. Far, far away, out beyond the kitchen window and past the Near Pasture, the lights of Mrs. Perley's house were probably still shining. The cup of tea was probably still warm beside her.

And then he heard his grandfather's voice. *Make do. Make do.*

The trouble was, what did he have to make do with right now?

Cooper crawled out from beneath the table, through the kitchen, through the hallway, on into the parlor, and up onto the couch. Quietly he lifted the window—as the glass in the kitchen door broke. Quietly he lifted up the screen—as another pane in the front door broke.

Climbing onto the sill, Cooper was filled with the overwhelming fear that someone was going to grab him from behind. He could almost feel iron hands clutching his ankle. He panicked and, instead of jumping out onto the grass, more or less tumbled out into his grandmother's prize hydrangea bushes—which would not be winning any blue ribbons this year now, he figured.

It was a lot colder out here—he could even see his breath. Maybe the Very Big Men could see his breath too. So step by step in the darkness, Cooper stayed close against the house, holding his arms around his chest, trying not to breathe. He heard the kitchen door open and close, then the low muttering of voices using words his grandmother would never have let his grandfather use in her house. Through the window, he saw two beams of light crisscrossing the room.

Actually, it was a whole lot colder out here; Cooper shivered and was surprised to find that when he was this cold, his teeth really did chatter. Trying to keep them still, he followed the house around to the side door. He opened it—oiling its hinges was one of the things his grandfather must have done while he was at school—and took down one of the red flannel shirts his grandfather kept for cold morning milkings. He smelled him as he put it on, and the weight of the wool was like the weight of his grandfather's hands on his shoulders. Somehow he felt that now he'd be able to make do.

He went back outside. The pastel moon hadn't come up yet, and it was as dark as could be—except for up the hill at Mrs. Perley's, where the lights were still shining. Almost everything in him willed his legs to start running up there, and with bare feet he'd be quiet enough that the Very Big Men wouldn't hear him over the humming of the sedan.

The humming of the sedan.

That was when the one part of him that wasn't wanting his legs to start running took over. There were at least two Very Big Men in his grandparents' house. In his house.

And they didn't belong there.

He held his grandfather's shirt close around him and looked up once more at Mrs. Perley's. Then he hunched down and ran across to the sedan. As quiet as starlight, he opened the driver's door and looked in. Nothing too complicated. Maybe the seats were made of leather, and maybe the dashboard did have more dials than a fighter jet plane. But it didn't smell like a real car. It didn't even have a clutch. He reached in and turned the steering wheel until the tires followed the driveway. Then he hit the door lock, put the car into gear, and slammed the door as hard as he could.

And then he ran back around the corner of the house and toward the Big Barn.

The result was everything he could have hoped for.

Satisfying hollers erupted from the house—louder even than the grinding of the tires on the gravel driveway. Probably the sedan wasn't dawdling any—Cooper had known by the hum that the idle was set way too high. It was probably moving down the gravel pretty well, and probably faster than the Very Big Men could run. Cooper figured it would hold the driveway for a bit, but there was that bend halfway up to the road that the car would come to any—well, there it was. He heard a crunch as the car left the gravel, two twangs as it veered through the electric fence, and a soft squish as it plowed into the Near Pasture—where his grandfather had spread a good load of manure not so long ago.

Cooper was shivering and sweating at the same time as he sprinted back to his house and up to the kitchen door. He was almost there when he heard breaking glass and figured the Very Big Men had gotten into the sedan. Then he heard wheels spinning and probably throwing back stuff they weren't used to throwing back.

He couldn't help but smile.

He got into the kitchen, careful not to step on the broken glass—something else to fix now, along with the phone and the electric and the top porch step. Though maybe he should let the top porch step be. It was almost as good as a barking dog.

Shivering hard now, he moved through the hallway, his arms still holding his grandfather's flannel shirt around himself, and looked out the front parlor window. He couldn't see the sedan, but he could see where it had come out through the fence in the Near Pasture.

Another thing to fix. Dang.

And that was when he felt a hand grab his shoulder. And another grab his right arm and jerk it quickly and easily behind his back, so hard and high that he felt his muscles almost tear. His grandfather's shirt was pulled over his head, and he was dragged back from the window. He held himself up on his toes to relieve some of the tearing. But it didn't help.

He was turned, and a light flashed against his covered face, shining through the flannel. It dazzled his eyes, so that he couldn't see anything but white.

"Birth certificate," said a low voice.

"Get off—"

His arm was twisted, and he felt like his elbow was about to pop out of joint. The tearing in his arm began to burn. The white in his eyes didn't seem to be coming only from the flashlight. He wondered if he was about to pass out.

The flashlight lowered and jabbed into his stomach— but he couldn't bend forward with his arm held back.

"Birth certificate," said the low voice again.

"Under the mattress. My room upstairs," he said. He hardly recognized his own voice.

The arm untwisted just a little, and Cooper heard heavy feet on the stairs. On the stairs of his grandparents' house. Dang, they were right there in his own house!

"Who—" he began, but immediately his arm was

twisted again, and he cried out at the sudden searing pain.

A moment later, the heavy feet came back, and he was thrown down. He just barely got his left arm in front of his face before it struck the floor. He lay there, not moving, unable to gather his right arm back around in front of him, breathing sharply, waiting to see something in his eyes besides the white of the pain. The front door closed, and the top porch step groaned. He waited for the sound of the sedan driving off, but he could not hear it over the throbbing of his heart.

He felt himself sway, then slide over onto his side. His arm was still behind his back when he fell into the white of his eyes and lost consciousness.

Mrs. Perley slept late that morning because of her cold, so it was Mr. Searle who found him, having fumed up from the Big Barn when Cooper didn't show up for morning milking. Mr. Searle gently brought his arm back around, helped him onto the parlor couch, and rubbed some of the pain out of his shoulder with the grip of a dairyman. All the while that Cooper told him about the midnight visit, Mr. Searle didn't say a thing.

Cooper flexed his arm, amazed that the muscles hadn't been ripped up after all. "I guess it works all right," he said.

"Maybe so, but you won't be no good today. I'll finish up the milking. Probably have to do evening milking by myself too."

"I'll be fine by then."

"As if Mrs. Perley will let you milk after this. As if she'd let you lift a single thing."

They heard the front door open and Mrs. Perley's voice in the front hallway. "Gracious goodness, what has happened to this glass?"

"As if she won't give you a talking-to if she walks in right now with you wearing only shorts with a lady in the house."

So Mr. Searle went out and brought Mrs. Perley down to the kitchen, and Cooper got upstairs, every step somehow throbbing in his shoulder. There were four more gracious goodnesses that reached him—each one louder than the last—but by the time he came back to the kitchen the worst was past, and Mrs. Perley was loading up the dining room table while she watched for him.

"Come eat before it gets cold," she said, a bit shrill.

While they ate, she fussed at Mr. Searle. "Why did you not come up earlier, you and your dairyman's sense, you old fraud?"

And she fussed at Cooper. "Do not use that arm until I say otherwise."

And she fussed at herself. "I knew that I should have stayed the night. Whatever would Edna have said if she knew?"

Cooper and Mr. Searle were silent, knowing there wasn't any talk that would withstand the assault. After breakfast, Mr. Searle looked awfully glad to escape to the cows. Cooper, meanwhile, wished he were there with him, instead of driving into New Lincoln in Mrs. Perley's Plymouth to see Sheriff Gibbs—again.

★ ★ ★ ★ ★ ★ ★ ★ ★

# CHAPTER FIVE

Sheriff Gibbs's office was full of furniture left over from state budget cuts, all gathered around a sort of gray carpet that had been worn through before Dwight D. Eisenhower came through New Lincoln looking for New Hampshire votes. But the pictures on the wall were new; every one was of Sheriff Gibbs, shaking the governor's hand or the lieutenant governor's hand or someone else's hand—even Senator Wickham's hand. Cooper looked at that one closely. Senator Wickham looked plain-out bored; Sheriff Gibbs was grinning to the edges of his face.

He was about as helpful as he had been the first time. He rubbed his considerable chin while Cooper told him about the phone, the flashlight, the two men, the car he sent into the Near Pasture, his arm, and the birth certificate.

"Huh," said Sheriff Gibbs slowly at the end. "That's quite a story." He leaned way back in his chair, so far that Cooper wondered how the whole contraption didn't fall over. "Did you remember to break the glass from the outside in, so it would look like someone was coming in that way?"

"What?" said Cooper.

"And the same with the back door too?"

"Are you saying I broke my own windows?"

"See," said the sheriff to Mrs. Perley, "I always knew that they only take the quickest and brightest at New Lincoln High." He turned to Cooper. "Listen, son, you've had a bad few days. And you're not all that sure what's going to happen to you now. But I have to tell you, what you're saying just doesn't make any sense."

"I have known Cooper all his life," said Mrs. Perley. "He would never make up something like this."

"After all he's been through, I'd be surprised if he didn't come up with a whopper or two." Sheriff Gibbs looked at Cooper. "It does get him a whole lot of attention, doesn't it? That and a fire and some sort of break-in, and who knows what'll be next."

"What about the electricity and the phone? They're both dead. Did I do that too?"

"It's dangerous to play around electricity, son. Didn't Mrs. Perley teach you that back in fifth grade?"

"There's the skid marks on the driveway," said Cooper. "And the break where they went through the electric and into the Near Pasture."

The sheriff pushed back even farther. Even farther! "You been driving again, Cooper?"

"I wouldn't drive into my own field."

"Your grandpa once told me you drove into your own mailbox. That true?"

"I wouldn't drive into my own field."

"Huh," said Sheriff Gibbs.

"Raymond Gibbs—"

"Mrs. Perley, just listen to the boy talk. Wires cut. Big men breaking in. Glass broken. Phone dead. Electric dead. Black sedans driving off into a field. An arm almost torn off. He's a kid from New Lincoln. This isn't some spy mystery. All this story about some intruder and a birth certificate. What would anybody want with his birth certificate? Does that sound reasonable to you?"

"Reasonable has nothing at all to do with it. It happened," said Mrs. Perley.

Sheriff Gibbs smiled again. "Reasonable has everything to do with it. Reasonable is whether I go out on a wild goose chase or serve the people of this good town

★ 75 ★

by working right here." Sheriff Gibbs put his feet up on the desk.

"I never told you that the car was a black sedan," said Cooper.

Suddenly, the sheriff's office grew absolutely still.

"Mrs. Perley must have told me," said the sheriff slowly.

"No," said Mrs. Perley, "I did not."

Cooper wrapped his arms around himself.

"Then I suppose, Mrs. Perley, I'm brighter than you took me for back in fifth grade."

"You would have to be clairvoyant," she said. "Are you clairvoyant, Raymond?"

Cooper could tell right away that Sheriff Gibbs had no idea what *clairvoyant* meant. He himself didn't know. But he did know enough to back away when the sheriff took his feet down and drew himself up.

"Son, you can't stay on a farm alone. As soon as you leave—and you better be leaving to go back to school—I'll be calling New Hampshire Social Services to turn this over to them."

"It's my farm now."

"No one's disputing that yet. But until this all gets sorted out, I'm sure Mr. Searle—"

"Sure, Mr. Searle will be glad to take over the farm," said Cooper. "But I'm not leaving."

"They'll be arranging for someone to pick you up. It's for your own good."

"Cooper is fine where he is," said Mrs. Perley.

Now the sheriff came around his desk. His hands were clenching and unclenching, like a gunfighter in an old Western.

"Neither of you has any idea what you're getting mixed up in," he said, and it was as if his voice had become as cold as Fright. "Not one single idea." He looked hard at Cooper. "Life isn't always what you expect it to be. Sometimes it can be full of surprises."

"I've seen surprises," said Cooper. "I'll make do."

Mrs. Perley put her arm around him.

"We'll see how long that lasts." Sheriff Gibbs turned back to Mrs. Perley. "And maybe you'd better stay up in your own house. This isn't New Lincoln Elementary anymore."

"Do not begin a sentence with a conjunction, Raymond. It is grammatically improper," said Mrs. Perley.

Sheriff Gibbs went back around his desk. "Thank you for the visit," he said. "I'll be sure to type up a report and get right on the case—Raging Birth Certificate Thief on the Loose." He sat down and put his feet up on the desk again. He rubbed his chin and clasped his hands on his belly, over which there was a lot to clasp. "New Lincoln police, always at your service," he said.

Outside the sheriff's office, Mrs. Perley stood by her Plymouth with her key in her hand. "He certainly is a most unpleasant man—as helpful as a thunderstorm during a Sunday school picnic. What did he mean by accusing you of making up the entire story?" She spoke more and more quickly and waved the key at Cooper. "What did he mean by that? And how did he know about the black sedan? Drat!" She punched her hand into the air. "See how upset he has made me? I've begun a sentence with a conjunction myself. And he's made me say *drat*. Oh, and there I go again with another conjunction!"

"I won't ever tell," said Cooper.

"Thank you. And drat the man anyway."

Mrs. Perley drove Cooper back home at about fifteen miles an hour. "With all the excitement and with the damage done to your arm—no, no, Cooper, do not deny it, I have seen the way you hold it—you can miss one day of school," she said. "Hold on tightly," and she drove down the hill and past the Hurd place.

Cooper didn't argue about school. Besides, now that the Ancient Egyptian Trade Routes had been finally mapped, there was a new report on the Incan ruins of Machu Picchu he had to work on. He didn't think he could get himself all worked up over another ancient pile, but he hoped that maybe Mr. Hupfer would accept an early report on Machu Picchu along with his late Ancient Egyptian Trade Route map and call it even.

So Cooper came home, had a raspberry tart, and settled into the day. It turned out to be the first of a solid run of quiet days, and Cooper figured that he had earned them.

One day was pretty much like another. He met Mr. Searle at the Big Barn for milking each morning. He ate oatmeal with brown sugar—more brown sugar than his grandmother used to let him have—just before he rode to school. He endured New Lincoln High School. He ran cross. After he got home, he checked the Big Barn, which was always mucked out—some days more proper than others—then took the Farmall to mow the Orchard. He tended his grandmother's vegetable garden; it was time for digging up potatoes. Afterward, Mr. Searle would be up to grumble during evening milking. Then back to the house, where Mrs. Perley had supper for the both of them. Then homework, mostly the Machu Picchu report, while Mrs. Perley made his lunch for the next day—she especially favored salami and cream cheese sandwiches. And then late, just before bedtime, they watched the news, where Hannah Joyce reported on Senator Wickham's sinking numbers in New Hampshire's voting polls. They would smile together.

Cooper was surprised at how quickly his life came to feel somehow normal.

Except at school.

From the moment he stepped into New Lincoln High, it seemed that he had been marked as the Boy Who

Was About to Leave. Ms. Dove smiled widely every time she saw him, as if he were a sacrifice about to be offered up for the greater good of the school. If he helped Senator Wickham win the election, who knew how grateful the President of the United States might be to New Lincoln High? Who knew what grants and funding and computers and television monitors and what-all would appear in trucks backing up to the high school loading dock, trucks with "U.S. Government" printed on the side? Every time she looked at him, Cooper felt she was looking at dollar signs. Lots of them.

Mr. Hupfer had suddenly begun to make speeches about those who thought they could get through life without reading a book or who thought that running around the country "experiencing" was as good as formal learning, which, he said, was the great deception of our age and probably the reason the ancient Incans of Machu Picchu died out.

Coach had given up warning his runners about Admiral Ames Root Beer. Now, at the end of eleven-mile runs, as the team leaned over, barely breathing, with their hands on their knees, Coach shook his head sadly and mourned for those who would start a training regimen and then give it up. They would grow fat and lazy, he said, and the "liptodes" in their bodies would start to gel and lose their cellular walls and likely dissolve into some sort of protoplasm that floated around in your body until they all came together in your heart—and we all know what that means.

Peter just punched him in the shoulder most mornings. "Glad you're still here."

"I'm not going anywhere."

"There really is something wrong with you. A chance to get out of school for who knows how long. Going around on a campaign. Maybe they'd even let you drive a 1958 Ford in some parade. But I'm glad you're still here anyway. There's got to be someone who comes in three minutes behind me every race."

"Three minutes," said Cooper. "Try thirty-five seconds."

"We all have our dreams," Peter said and ducked when Cooper swung at him.


*We all have our dreams,* thought Cooper, lying in bed at night. He would listen as the quiet of the house came on around him. There were none of the sounds of his grandfather watching television, of him closing the windows against the night air. Cooper did not hear him going out one more time to check the barns or coming back in and locking the front door and then the kitchen door. Or climbing the steps to bed.

There was none of the muffled talk of his grandfather and grandmother in their room.

Every night, Cooper listened only to the quiet, looking

out his window at the tilting stars. And loneliness like night darkened him through the late days of September and on into chilled October.

It was cold enough now that in the mornings, before he went out to milk, Cooper started up the woodstove from the night's embers. When he had a blaze going and the dry-iron smell of the heat began to fill the room, Mrs. Perley came out and put on a pot of water to boil. They sat together in the dark, the only light from the woodstove, with no failed silences, and Mrs. Perley made them both cups of tea with honey in Cooper's grandmother's best company teapot. Cooper didn't care if it wasn't a proper dairyman's way; it was good to have something warm in his gut when he went out to milk.

But what he did care about—and what made the broken part deep within him twist every time he thought of it—was what Senator Wickham had told him about Mr. Searle. Every time he saw him in the barn or by the house or walking through the Orchard, he wondered if Mr. Searle was assessing the value of the property.

So one day, after evening milking, he asked him.

"You figure on taking over this place?"

Mr. Searle looked at him. "I already got a place," he said.

"Senator Wickham told me you own this place too."

Mr. Searle finished rinsing the hose, then curled it up neatly into its cabinet.

"Do you own this place too?" asked Cooper.

Mr. Searle picked up the next hose. He held it, then pushed his hat back and took a deep breath. "Senator Wickham has a big mouth, and the stuff coming out of it ain't his business at all." He sighed. "Mrs. Perley told me you'd be wanting to know someday. She said you just wouldn't let it rest. I guess she was right. So the truth is, Eli Jewett were a fine dairyman, none better. But Eli Jewett were also a terrible businessman, none worse. Every year he ended up with more debt than cash, and he never could see his way out of that."

"So you lent him money," said Cooper.

"Some."

"A lot of money."

Mr. Searle shrugged. "Enough so he could get by."

"How much did he pay back?"

Mr. Searle began to rinse the hose again.

"None," said Cooper. "So the farm is yours."

Mr. Searle stacked the hose on top of the other one in the cabinet. "They didn't leave you a whole lot, boy."

The broken part twisted fiercely in Cooper's gut.

Riding into school that morning, Cooper wondered if Mr. Searle owned all the cows—Star and Moon especially. At New Lincoln High, he wondered if Mr. Searle owned the Farmall. During cross practice, he wondered if Mr. Searle owned the house. (He came in six and a half minutes behind Peter.) When he closed the barn doors after evening milking that night, he wondered if they belonged to Mr. Searle too. If the grass he was walking on belonged to Mr. Searle. If the front porch and the groaning top step belonged to Mr. Searle.

"Whatever you are, you're too young to run a dairy farm alone," Mr. Searle had told him the day of the funeral. Maybe what he meant to say was that he was too young to run Mr. Searle's dairy farm.

"Dang," he said out loud, and tried to remember that New Hampshire dairymen don't have a tear in them. But then again, he didn't know how much longer he was going to be a New Hampshire dairyman.

He wondered if one day Hannah Joyce would report on him losing his farm.

Maybe he should give it all up and head out on the campaign trail—like everyone seemed to want.

That night, Cooper watched the moon tussle with the branches of his grandmother's russet apple tree until it floated away free and threw its silver gleaming all across the Near Pasture, and he wept—even if a dairy-man wasn't supposed to.

By mid-October, Cooper's running time was becoming—and Coach was trying to be kind—"ugly." At meets on

Saturdays, Peter was the only one still standing on the sidelines to clap him in at the end of the race—a race Peter had finished ten or twelve minutes earlier. Cooper staggered more than ran the last mile.

*Stagger* was a word Hannah Joyce was using a lot lately too—about Senator Wickham. The voting polls put him so far behind the President, she said, that it would take a miracle for him to recover. Either that, or something terrible would have to happen to the President's campaign, and voters would turn to Senator Wickham as the only alternative. But, she said, shaking her head to viewers of the late-night news, no one could imagine what that might be.

But sometimes miracles do happen. And during the last week of October, two came almost back-to-back.

The first was announced by Hannah Joyce, and even Cooper and Mrs. Perley, who were sort of sleepy at the time, paid attention.

"There are unconfirmed reports tonight that the America for Wickham campaign has obtained documents that—and please remember these are unconfirmed reports—documents that suggest a scandal in the President's earlier life has been hushed up for a decade—perhaps longer. Senator Wickham has yet to confirm the report, but sources close to him are saying the scandal could end not only the President's campaign for re-election, but the current administration.

The White House is dismissing the reports as 'the desperate acts of a desperate man,' but it is not commenting on the substance of the reports." Hannah Joyce paused and looked seriously at the camera. "What this means for the New Hampshire campaign is still unknown at this time."

"Gracious goodness," said Mrs. Perley. And what more was there to say after that?

The second miracle came three days later, after the last freshman cross meet of the season, on a day bright as Goodness and warm as Hope.

Cooper had come in so far behind in his race that the leaders from the next race had passed him—and they were from New Lincoln Middle School. It had been more than a little humiliating. When the bus dropped him off after the meet, Cooper couldn't even look at Coach as he climbed down. He knew he'd be running the bleachers in PE the next day. The bus pulled away, and in the combusting fumes he slung his bag over his shoulder and started up the driveway. Then he stopped. Where Mrs. Perley usually parked her Plymouth, there was a jeep. And sitting on the top porch step was a man with large legs, large hands, and large neck, dressed in a suit perfectly tailored from elegant lapels to creased cuffs.

He stood up on his huge legs, and the top porch step groaned in relief. He came down the steps, and Cooper walked up, dropping his bag and very aware of his very sweaty uniform. He held out his hand when Mr. Heavy Legs held out his.

"Mrs. Perley has been called up to Keene," Mr. Heavy Legs said. "Some emergency about her university alumni association."

"So who are you?" asked Cooper.

"I saw you run today, kid," said Mr. Heavy Legs. "You were terrible."

"Thanks."

"You're welcome."

And then came the second miracle of the month.

"You aren't nearly as good as your father was," Mr. Heavy Legs said.

The world stopped spinning. Every single living creature in it kept still. The wind halted, clouds slowed, and the sun held its breath.

"My father?" Cooper whispered.

"He went to State four years in a row in high school. Went to Nationals twice. He never did win, but he was one of the best anyone in our town had ever seen."

"My father," Cooper whispered again.

"Kid, I've been sent to bring you to see someone. Someone important. Go on inside and get cleaned up. Then we'll go."

But Cooper felt the eyes of Senator Wickham moving

down the rows in the auditorium. And he felt the eyes in the cameras in the barn—cameras that he hadn't been able to find yet. *Was this another set of eyes?* he wondered. He picked up his bag. "You knew my father?"

"Stay focused, kid. You need to come with me."

"So I can see Senator Wickham again."

Mr. Heavy Legs pointed inside. "Hurry up," he said.

Cooper took a step back. "All I have to do is drop this and run."

"You forget, kid. I've seen you run. I could take you."

"You don't look so fast."

"The reason your father didn't win Nationals," said Mr. Heavy Legs, "was that I did. By a lot."

"And then what? So you catch me. Then comes the arm behind the back routine again? Some more papers you want? Maybe last year's report card?"

Mr. Heavy Legs shook his head. "I've seen that report card, kid. I wouldn't be too proud of it. Go on and get cleaned up. Someone's waiting to see you."

"Who?"

"Someone very important."

"And he wants something."

Mr. Heavy Legs nodded. "Most people do."

"Then tell him to get in line," said Cooper. "Mr. Searle wants the farm. Senator Wickham wants me on the campaign trail. Sheriff Gibbs wants New Hampshire Social Services to take me away. Ms. Dove wants to trade me for computers. And Mr. Hupfer wants a report on Machu Picchu."

"I've been there, Machu Picchu. It's worth a report. If I had time, I'd tell you about it. But I don't have time."

"And there was the fire. Did you set that? You know, that fire scared the cows, and scared cows don't give milk the whole next day."

"I'm all cut up about that, kid. But I didn't set it."

"You can tell Senator Wickham I'm not going to help him."

"I'll be sure to do that first thing."

"And you can tell him that no one around here trusts him as far as they can throw him."

"You've all got good taste."

"And I'm not going anywhere."

Mr. Heavy Legs sighed. "You've got guts, kid, maybe even brains. But guts and brains aren't what I'm looking for."

"I'm all cut up about that," said Cooper.

Mr. Heavy Legs shook his head. "Your father was a lot easier to get along with."

Cooper said nothing.

"Look, kid. No one is forcing you to do anything. But if you don't come with me, it's a mistake. Maybe a big mistake. And where I come from, people usually don't recover from mistakes. They just go away and aren't heard from again."

"Tell Senator Wickham I'm not leaving this farm. It's all I have."

Mr. Heavy Legs walked past Cooper and got into the jeep. He turned on the ignition and backed up to Cooper. He handed him a card with a single phone number on it. "I'm not forcing you to come, kid. Not yet. But things are going to start happening fast. Very fast. Call if you want me. And one thing more: Next time I see you, I won't be *asking* you to come."

"Do you know what happened to my father?"

"Of course I do," said Mr. Heavy Legs. "He died in a car accident."

Then he drove away.

★ ★ ★ ★ ★ ★ ★ ★ ★

# Chapter Six

Mrs. Perley came back from Keene later that afternoon, fussing and fuming about so-called university alumni association meetings that never had been planned at all. "Whatever were they thinking, having me drive all the way down to Keene for no good reason? Whatever were they thinking?"

Cooper did not tell her about Mr. Heavy Legs. She seemed upset enough for one day.

And besides, it all sounded so impossible, like something you would read in a book. He wondered if Mrs. Perley might look at him the way Sheriff Gibbs did, thinking that maybe, after all, Cooper wasn't telling the truth but was just coming up with one outlandish story after another.

So he didn't say anything about Mr. Heavy Legs.

And he wondered if he really had known his father.

And he wondered who Mr. Heavy Legs wanted to take him to see.

All that wondering wasn't helping his Machu Picchu report. He had given up hope of handing it in early; now he figured that just meeting the deadline was a sign of steadiness and dependability and maybe Mr. Hupfer would be impressed enough with that to forgive the late Ancient Egyptian Trade Routes map.

"Are you making progress on the Machu Picchu report?" Mr. Hupfer asked on the last of the yellow October days.

Cooper nodded. "I guess."

"You guess," said Mr. Hupfer. "Tell me, Cooper, who is Hiram Bingham?"

"Hiram Bingham?"

"Yes."

"Hiram Bingham."

Mr. Hupfer sighed. "I'm not going to get another late project, am I?"

"No, sir."

"Cross practice is over now. You've got some more time. Get going on it."

"I'm already pretty far along."

"Then you know that Hiram Bingham is the discoverer of Machu Picchu."

It was, Cooper told Peter later, as humiliating as finishing after the leaders of a middle school cross race.

But it is hard to write about ancient ruins that no one has lived in for a thousand years when you're worried about how long you'll be living in your own house. And if Sheriff Gibbs or Mr. Searle, maybe, or Ms. Dove or Senator Wickham or maybe even Mr. Heavy Legs had their way, he wasn't going to be around much longer.

And who would milk Moon and Star by hand then?

As Cooper coasted down to his house that yellow afternoon, the wind in his spokes sounded mournful, and Cooper looked at the house and tried to fix it in his mind like a painting that would never leave him. But its beauty was so thick and so real that it could never be just a painting. The sun was tilting down, backlighting the copper leaves on the oaks and throwing the front of the house into cool shadow. The barn was so red, and the trees on the hills beyond still so golden; the cows lolling in the Far Pasture were so still. It was all as he had seen it every day, coming home from school. But it had never before seemed so fragile. Cooper held his breath.

He wasn't up to the house yet when Mrs. Perley came hustling onto the porch—hustling, that is, as well as she could. "Is everything all right?" she called.

Cooper nodded. "Mrs. Perley, you don't have to watch for me every day."

"Edna would want me to be watching for you."

She was, Cooper knew, exactly right. He thought suddenly of how losing the farm would mean losing Mrs. Perley too, and he was surprised at how much the broken part inside him tightened. He put his arm around her, and they stood together quietly. He told her about Machu Picchu, and she told him about an afternoon of phone calls.

"I believe Sheriff Gibbs was going to call New Hampshire Social Services to see about your case. But I have not been retired so long that I am without influence myself. So I called Social Services for the county, and then for the region, and then for the state. They would tell me nothing. All they would say is that your case record is restricted—but they would not tell me by whom it was restricted."

"So what does that mean?"

She shook her head. "Perhaps if we knew that, we would also know why it is that there seems to be no record at all of your birth anywhere in New Hampshire— or anywhere in New England. I called everywhere it might be. There was no notation in state records anywhere. There was no sign of it in county records, or even at Keene Memorial Hospital, where your grandparents said you were born."

"That just means my parents were living somewhere outside of New England. No big mystery."

"No, I suppose not," said Mrs. Perley. "I have probably made a dozen phone calls all for nothing. I had better go get something for us to eat."

But Cooper knew she was not convinced that there was no big mystery, and so he too began to wonder why there wasn't a single record of his birth anywhere except in the folder marked *Cooper Jewett* that had once been in his grandfather's desk.

And that was now somewhere else.

At milking time, Mr. Searle was not up to the barn, and Cooper smiled in satisfaction. He had missed only the one day his arm had almost been torn off, but here was Mr. Searle, late.

He climbed to the loft and brought down the bales for the cows—a little extra for Moon and Star. While they set to munching, he set to milking, and he finished before Mr. Searle got there. He brought the milk to the cooler and then ran inside for supper. Mrs. Perley fussed over Mr. Searle not being there. She called down to his house, but the phone rang without him picking up.

"You would think he would let us know when he goes out," she said.

She made a plate for him and put it into the oven to keep warm. But he never did come up, this Farnham Searle who wanted his farm—and Cooper was just as glad.

After supper, Cooper went back out to the Big Barn, climbed onto the Farmall—he had done it a thousand times with his grandfather behind him—and loaded up the spreader to take the manure out to the Far Pasture. He'd have time for only a couple of loads, since the sun was already set and drawing the day down after it. So it was almost dark when out of the corner of his eye Cooper saw Mr. Searle down the hill, waving. But he wouldn't look toward Mr. Searle. Not toward the man who wanted his farm. He focused on the manure instead.

He finished the loads, unhitched the spreader, and brought the tractor around back, under the shed. He checked on the cows and pulled the Big Barn door to. Heading up to the house, he looked down the hill once more.

It was hard to see in the gathering dark, but it looked like Mr. Searle was on the ground.

Cooper watched another minute.

Mr. Searle didn't move.

Cooper began to run, and when he reached him, it was barely light enough to make out that Mr. Searle's ruddy face was pale, his white shirt was stained with blood, and one arm was bent behind his back.

"Mr. Searle," he cried.

"I'm woozy, that's all," said Mr. Searle. "Don't fuss."

"There's blood all over you."

Mr. Searle looked down at his shirt, as if he was just

understanding that for the first time. "Oh, the dickens. Get me down to my house." But Mr. Searle was woozy enough that he wasn't going to stand.

Cooper sprinted back to his house, hollered for Mrs. Perley, and rushed up to his grandparents' bedroom. He grabbed the quilt from the cedar chest and ran back down the stairs. In the Big Barn, he threw the quilt into the tow, brought the Farmall around, and hitched it. By the time he was down to Mr. Searle, Mrs. Perley was kneeling beside him, holding his one bent arm.

"Mr. Searle, I'm going to get you in the tow now," said Cooper.

"That Farmall is missing," said Mr. Searle.

"I know."

Cooper got Mr. Searle sitting up, then standing—sort of—and finally into the tow. Mrs. Perley climbed in next to him, holding the quilt around him. Cooper brought them down to Mr. Searle's house, looking back most of the time to be sure he wasn't falling off.

"I'm all right," grumbled Mr. Searle, but he was breathing hard. "A knock or two isn't going to kill a New Hampshire dairyman." Still, he had trouble on the back porch stairs, and his right knee kept going out while they crossed the kitchen. "I've had a lot worse broke than just a nose," he said, as Cooper let him down on a chair. "A whole lot worse, let me tell you."

Mr. Searle's kitchen was considerably dingier than

Cooper's grandparents'. Cooper wasn't sure how many meals it had taken to leave that many dishes in the sink, but more than a few. The wall calendar had needed changing for two seasons—actually, when Cooper looked closer at it, for a year and two seasons. And apparently Mr. Searle liked to keep things handy, since boxes of instant cereal and Minute Rice and ready-to-microwave stuffing, cans of peas and corn and peaches, and bags of flour and sugar crowded the dishes by the sink. Baskets of carrots and potatoes huddled in the corners, the dirt still on them.

But there was something more. The kitchen door hung from only one hinge, and two of the chairs were smashed. There were smears of blood across the linoleum.

Cooper found a clean towel—this wasn't easy—and moved the dishes aside to wet it. "How'd you break your nose?" Cooper came back to Mr. Searle and began to wash the blood off his cheek.

"It wasn't a cow, be sure of that. The day hasn't dawned when a cow could kick me."

Cooper reflected that plenty of those days had dawned for him.

"Two guys in sixteen-piece suits."

Cooper went very cold.

"Asking questions they hadn't any right to be asking."

Mrs. Perley took the towel and began to wipe Mr. Searle's cheek.

"Questions about what?" Cooper asked.

"Questions about what I am going to tell you right now."

"Farnham, it is not our place," said Mrs. Perley.

"Of course it's not our place. But if not us, then whose dang place is it? There's no one else to tell him, unless you count the Methodist parson. But someone has to tell him. He may be on the young side, but he's a dairy-man, through and through, and he's got a right to know what's what."

"You old goat," said Mrs. Perley. "You are still bleeding."

"Of course I'm still bleeding. My nose is broke. Broken noses bleed."

"What am I supposed to know?" asked Cooper.

Mr. Searle glared at Mrs. Perley.

"You have to tell him now," she said, "though I am not sure that anything good will come of it."

Mr. Searle turned to Cooper, blood still smeared across his face. He looked like an ancient pirate. "Maybe it's not my place. But Eli and your grandmother never spoke about it. Afraid word would get around. Afraid you'd hear it from someone, I suppose."

"Hear what?"

Mr. Searle glared at him now. "What I'm about to tell you if you stop asking questions."

"I'll stop asking questions." Cooper held his breath.

"You were just a baby, no more than a couple of weeks old, when you got brought to the Jewetts' farm."

"I know," said Cooper. "My parents. Then there was the car accident."

"Not your parents," said Mr. Searle. "And are you going to be quiet or not?"

Cooper didn't say anything.

"A man drove up to the farm, and your grandmother came out. He said he was in some kind of emergency, his wife was hurt, he had to find a place to leave the baby for a couple of hours, and the minister down at New Lincoln Methodist had given him her name."

"So she took you," said Mrs. Perley.

"And that was the very first time Edna Jewett ever laid eyes on you," said Mr. Searle. "You were homely and smelled to high heaven when I first saw you. Never could tell what made Edna take to you so almighty much. Never could figure what made Eli take to you either. But there he was, running down to the A&P for diapers and formula and blankets, even though it was just for a couple of hours."

"And when the man came back?" asked Cooper so quietly that Mr. Searle didn't fuss at him for asking another question.

"Never did come back. Eli called down to New Lincoln Methodist, but they'd never heard of any man and baby. Week later, medical records from Keene

Memorial showed up in the mail, with all the names and addresses scratched out, except for your first name, and a letter saying they were sorry but as how they couldn't keep you or some such rubbish."

Cooper nodded.

"Eli told me and Mrs. Perley all about it. I told him they needed to call someone up in the county offices, dang-fool business. But they'd never had children in the house, and your grandmother was so happy that he couldn't bear to have you taken away from her. I guess we all got used to you being around pretty quick. So the story just kind of grew up that there was a car accident, and they were going to raise you. Edna smiled so much, no one ever asked about it."

All those times late at night when Cooper had wondered about his folks. All those times he had imagined what they looked like, not having any pictures. All those times he had tried to figure out his ears and green eyes.

He had figured they were farm people.

But now who knew what they were?

Golly Moses, they might not even be from New Hampshire.

And they had just given him away. Just given him away like that.

All those times when he'd figured that their last thoughts had been of him.

He had never figured that they had just given him away to strangers.

He had never imagined his grandparents as strangers.

And then, he suddenly knew that if what Mr. Searle was telling him was true, he had two problems. Two very big problems.

One, since he wasn't a blood Jewett, he had no claim to the Jewett farm.

And, two, someone else wanted to know the story he had just heard. And that someone was willing to do a whole lot to find out. And he had no idea why.

Mr. Searle took back the towel. "Wish you hadn't used one of the good ones," he said to Mrs. Perley.

"There aren't any good ones," she said.

"How am I going to figure out who my parents were?" said Cooper.

Mr. Searle shrugged. "One thing's for sure," he said, "and I know this no matter how woozy I am: You living up on that farm, something's going to happen that nobody planned on. Not me, not Mrs. Perley, not Eli and Edna—not anybody."

"I've got nowhere else to go," said Cooper.

Mr. Searle finished wiping his face. "I suppose," he said.

They did not call Sheriff Gibbs about the two Very Big Men. What use would it have been?

★ 102 ★

But much later that night, after Mrs. Perley was asleep, Cooper came back downstairs and did make a phone call—to Mr. Heavy Legs.

He answered on the first ring.

"Bolster here."

"This is Cooper Jewett."

"What's happened, kid?"

"Bolster. That's a strange name."

"And Cooper isn't?"

"Most people are asleep right now. Not waiting by their phones."

"Don't be my mother, kid. You have something to tell me?"

"You sent two men to get a story out of Mr. Searle, didn't you? But you didn't get it."

"I don't send people. I work alone."

"They broke his nose and almost broke his arm—just like they did to me. So what is it exactly that you want?"

"Peace on earth, kid. What is it you want?"

"To be left alone."

A long pause. "I wish I could give you that, kid. I really do. But that isn't going to happen."

"Do you know how I came to this farm?"

"Yes."

"I do too."

"No," said Bolster slowly, "I don't think you do."

"My parents didn't die in a car accident, did they?"

Silence from Bolster. Then the phone went dead.

That night, Cooper turned all the lights on in the house. Even the bulb down in the cellar.

Mrs. Perley didn't say anything about it the next morning.

That next morning was a blessed Saturday. Cooper brought down the hay from the loft and fed it to the cows while milking. Mr. Searle didn't come up, so after he herded the cows out to the Far Pasture and mucked out proper, Cooper went down and milked for him. After lunch, he ran back down to Mr. Searle's to check on his nose and to borrow two new spark plugs for the Farmall. "You'll never get a Farmall running as smooth as a Silver King," said Mr. Searle, but by milking time Cooper had it running about as smooth as a tractor can run.

No one came from New Hampshire Social Services.

That night Cooper brought the hay down from the loft again, brought the cows in from the Far Pasture, and milked. By the time he and Mrs. Perley ate supper, which Mrs. Hurd had sent a pumpkin pie down for—a Mrs. Hurd pumpkin pie!—Cooper was dog-tired. They washed up the dishes together, standing at the kitchen sink and looking out the window, just like his grandmother had stood so many times.

He wondered if she ever used to watch for the man who had brought him to her.

Still no one from New Hampshire Social Services.

Sunday was pretty much the same, except that Mr. Searle came up dressed for services at New Lincoln Methodist. It was the first time Cooper had seen him wearing a tie, and Mr. Searle wasn't happy about it. "All this to listen to a Methodist parson."

He let Cooper tie it for him so that it didn't look like a noose.

Mrs. Perley eyed him with her hands on her hips. "This is an amazing thing, to see an old crumb bun like you on your way to church," she said.

"Someone has to keep an eye on this boy," said Mr. Searle.

Mrs. Perley drove her Plymouth. Very slowly.

"If we got out and crawled, we'd get there just as fast," said Mr. Searle. "You're just afraid of facing all those Methodists."

Mrs. Perley looked at him with Catholic pride. "Bring them on," she said.

They sat together all through the service, Reverend Hurd glancing now and then at Mr. Searle, who fidgeted with his tie, and at Mrs. Perley, who kept standing up and sitting down at all the wrong times, and at Cooper, who tried to keep a holy soberness about him. Afterward they all three had meat loaf with onions and brown gravy at the New Lincoln Diner—no dessert, since Mr. Searle was paying—and then stopped in at Cooper's house for the last three pieces of Mrs. Hurd's pumpkin pie.

"Not quite as sweet as it could be," said Mr. Searle.

"Neither are you," said Mrs. Perley.

Mr. Searle finished his pie in silence that worked, sort of.

Cooper finished his too. Afterward he left them sharing cups of tea with honey and walked outside. It was November and turning very cold now. Cooper was surprised at how quickly the maples had shaken their leaves off. The clouds were low and full, and if he looked hard enough, he could see a flake or two in the air. He wrapped his arms around his sides. *A November snow,* he thought, and went to fill the wood box.

He was right—by the next morning snow had brought down most of the rest of the maple leaves, and though the ground was still bare under the oaks, everywhere else it was covered.

With the snow, Cooper waited for the bus in the morning. It was late, but Cooper didn't mind. He stood at the end of his driveway, looking at his farm in the autumn snow. It was just as beautiful as in high summer—the snow piled softly on the porch railings, the Big Barn stark red against the white, his grandmother's chrysanthemums poking their jaunty yellow selves above the snow, and around it all the sweet smoke of maple wood rising from the chimney.

Good Lord, where would he go if this wasn't his farm?

He felt like Mr. Searle with a tie around his neck, strangling him. All through his morning classes, he kept pulling his collar out, until Peter asked, "You choking, Jewett?"

"No," said Mr. Hupfer, who always seemed to be listening. "He's trying to come down with something so that he can get an extension on the Machu Picchu report. Isn't that right, Cooper? But, Cooper, you would have to be diagnosed with a full-blown case of leprosy before that will happen. You have three days, and three days only."

Cooper felt like he really was strangling.

"Perhaps you could work after school with Peter here, who, if he did misjudge the flow of the Nile and omit the entire Red Sea in his Ancient Egyptian Trade Routes map, still gave a creditable effort."

Mr. Hupfer turned back to the board.

"Creditable effort," whispered Peter.

"Well, let me bow down and worship," said Cooper.

But that afternoon, Cooper did get off the bus with Peter, and together they went up to the bustle of the Hurd house. After Mrs. Hurd loaded them with fresh sugar cookies and milk, they got to work on Hiram

Bingham's journal and kept at it until they both figured they were within three days' sight of a creditable job on a Machu Picchu report.

"So now you don't have to come down with leprosy, Jewett," said Peter.

"I was thinking more along the lines of the Black Death."

"Too chancy. You might spread it around."

Cooper tried to think of something equally lethal but less contagious, but it was getting close to milking time, and Mrs. Hurd was calling them down to the kitchen and telling Peter to go outside to get Dorcas's gloves back on her. And while he did, Cooper waited, hoping for another blue-ribbon pumpkin pie from Mrs. Hurd.

But she didn't have a pie. She stood by the kitchen table in a room cleared of all other Hurds—which was a sight to see in the Hurd house.

"Mrs. Perley called last night," she said. "She told me that you know now about how you came to live with Eli and Edna."

Cooper nodded. "You knew too."

"Some," said Mrs. Hurd. "Fourteen years ago, Eli Jewett called us at the parsonage, asking if someone had come around the church with a baby that needed watching over. We hadn't heard a thing about it. Next

Sunday, here come Eli and Edna Jewett, bringing a baby into the nursery at New Lincoln Methodist, without a word of explaining."

"Reverend Hurd must have asked them."

"Of course. He went over that afternoon. Your grandfather showed him a letter from your parents, saying they weren't coming back for you. Reverend Hurd asked them what they were going to do, and your grandmother said that no one who left a baby like that had any right to ever come back. She marched over and took the letter, and before anyone could say a thing, she threw it in the woodstove."

"Was the letter signed?"

Mrs. Hurd put her hand on his arm. "I don't know, Cooper. If it was, there's no way of knowing now."

"They never told me," he said. "They never told me anything."

"Oh, Cooper, maybe they should have. Lord knows we should have told you sooner. And maybe we should have tried to find your parents. But if you could have seen your grandmother . . . if you could have seen her face . . ."

"They never told me anything," Cooper said again, his voice soft and quiet.

"They loved you. If you blame them for not telling you, you can't blame them very much."

"No," said Cooper. "But how do I know who I am now?"

Mrs. Hurd smiled and put her hands on his shoulders. "You are Cooper Jewett. You are a fine runner, a finer friend, and a moderate driver. You are a Methodist most Sundays. You are a dairyman every day. That's what it means to be Cooper Jewett."

The broken part in Cooper's gut tightened a little bit—but not much.

★ ★ ★ ★ ★ ★ ★ ★ ★

# CHAPTER SEVEN

LATE THAT AFTERNOON, Cooper walked around his house, and he walked around his fields and barn, and what he found was that every place he walked, Eli and Edna Jewett walked beside him.

While he retied the wire fence, there were his grandfather's hands next to his own. When he came up to the kitchen porch, there was his grandmother's voice to remind him to take his snowy boots off. When he stood by the Big Barn and looked down over the Far Pasture, he stood with his hands on his hips, just like his grandfather. When he brought in the last of the chrysanthemums and set them in a vase on the kitchen table, there was his grandmother smelling them. "Imagine," he could hear her say, "flowers from the snow."

Cooper felt about as lonely as a boy could feel.

But he knew where he belonged.

The snow melted, but every morning now, heavy frosts whitened the ground. Cooper dug up the rest of the potatoes, brought the McIntoshes down to the cellar, and stored a week's worth of wood by the kitchen porch. He kept a low fire in the woodstove all the time, and he and Mrs. Perley ate their supper in front of its yellow light, since it was warmer there than in the dining room. In the mornings, the fire was the first thing he tended to—before the cows. In the evenings, it was the last thing he tended to—after the cows.

And so the golden glow of autumn turned to the bright, cold sunlight of early winter, and it began to seem as if the black sedans had all been a dream. Which was fine. But what was not fine was that sometimes, especially when Cooper woke in the mornings, it began to seem that his grandparents had all been a dream, and their voices had gone with the night—and, sometimes, their faces too.

The report on Machu Picchu was finished, and Mr. Hupfer had, despite some verb problems, given it the kind of grade that Cooper would have brought home to show his grandparents. Instead, he showed it to Mrs. Perley, who bragged about it to Mr. Searle, who mentioned it to Cooper at the next morning milking.

"Heard you got an A on that Picchu Machu report of yours."

"Machu Picchu, and it was an A-minus."

"Never did set much store on learning about foreign places. Full of people who aren't from New Hampshire. Got enough to learn about right here. Didn't teach you to mend the electric. Didn't teach you to mend the phone line. You learn how to do that in New Hampshire."

"A lost city," whispered Cooper. "Jungles. Ruined temples. Buried gold! Wouldn't you like to see it?"

"Bucket," said Mr. Searle, handing him one. "Stool. Cow teat. No milk yet. Sure would like to see it."

That was the end of Machu Picchu.

At New Lincoln High School, Mr. Hupfer had tired of the ancient world too. He had turned to Current Affairs— most particularly, the upcoming New Hampshire primary, which, he said, "will decide the course of our nation for the next four years." So now when Cooper watched the ten o'clock news, slumped into the couch beside Mrs. Perley, he held a pad and pencil to take notes. He sat through bright and cheery commercials filled with bright and cheery people with smiles that were much too big and teeth that were way too white, until Hannah Joyce came on with the latest polls and the latest pictures of candidates campaigning up and down New Hampshire, smiling at folks and shaking their hands like old friends dropping in for dinner from Washington, D.C.

There was the President, standing at a podium down in Keene or riding in a motorcade through Concord or speaking at a high school gymnasium in Nashua, taking time out from being commander-in-chief to look into the problems of industrial waste coming up from Massachusetts and to try out the snowy slopes of the White Mountains. "Such a national resource will always be protected in this administration," the President promised, cheeks flushed with the cold air of the mountains.

Usually Mrs. Perley fell asleep about halfway through.

But after another bright and cheery commercial, there would be Senator Wickham, wearing a brand-spanking-new red flannel shirt and splitting cordwood for the cameras and still promising to support New Hampshire's families. "They will always find a friend in Washington, D.C., if I'm elected," he promised.

Cooper tried to hear his grandfather's voice. He knew just what he would say: "Coming into New Hampshire and talking like they know us in and out. Good Lord."

And Cooper tried to hear his grandmother chuckling from her rocker.

Every night he tried to hear their voices. Some nights he could. On those nights he couldn't, he went to bed sort of threadbare.

It was on one of those threadbare nights, halfway through November, that the voice of Senator Wickham suddenly became a whole lot louder than the disappearing voices of his grandparents.

The ten o'clock news began as it always did—bright and cheery. But almost immediately the announcer's voice came on urgently, as if something earth-shattering was up.

"Now, live, to a press conference with the America for Wickham campaign," said the announcer, and there was Senator Wickham striding up to the microphone, smiling like the nomination was already in his back pocket.

"Fellow American citizens," he began, "the values that we have held and cherished for generations, for which our fathers and forefathers died, are today under attack on fronts across our country—but nowhere are they under attack more than among those who have pledged to uphold those very values."

Cooper yawned. He put down his pencil. Maybe this wasn't going to be so all-fired urgent after all. He thought about the repair he'd made on the hose to the milking machine and wondered if he'd gotten the clamp tight enough.

And then, suddenly, he wasn't thinking about the clamp.

"I am here tonight," said Senator Wickham—he paused for a moment to look seriously at the cameras—"to announce to the people of New Hampshire, and to the people of the United States, a scandal in personal values that reaches to the heights of the White House itself. Rumors have already reached the press, but this campaign does not indulge in rumors. It looks for facts. And certain facts have now come to light that point to actions by the President that cut to the very heart of our most cherished social structure, the family. These are actions which speak to the worst in American politics—blind ambition that overwhelms love and loyalty. Some tangles are still to be unwound, but within a day or two, what has been a secret for fourteen years will be open to the entire country."

He nodded curtly, as if he'd said all that needed to be said.

But none of the reporters thought he'd said all that needed to be said. A flock of hands from the press rose up, and questions flew like scattering birds.

"Senator Wickham, could you tell us . . ."

"Senator, how did the President come to . . ."

"Senator!"

Senator Wickham nodded again and smiled. "Until the appropriate time, we ask the country's patience. An investigation this long in the making cannot and should not be rushed." Another flock of insisting hands came up. But Senator Wickham just shook his head, gathered his papers, and left with the questions still flying around him.

Hannah Joyce turned to the camera, held her microphone up, and shrugged. "It seems as if we're not to know—"

Cooper turned the television off. He thought of Senator Wickham and shivered.

He woke Mrs. Perley so she could go to her room—she'd missed Senator Wickham's announcement—and then he went around the house and turned on all the lights again, even the one in the cellar. *You never can be too sure,* he thought. Then he put on his coat and went out to check the Farmall and look into the Big Barn one more time. When he opened the door, the low, warm sounds the cows made were like the sounds of his own heart. He walked inside, and one by one, he stroked each of the sixty-four muzzles, the way his grandfather had done. The cows all looked up at him, eyes half-closed with the pleasure of the strokes.

But he felt lonely and threadbare.

When he turned to go back to the house, Bolster was standing by Moon and Star, his long black coat wrapped elegantly around him.

"Never did like farming myself," he said. "Too much work. Too dirty. Too cold. All those cows always wanting to be milked. I never did see the charm in it."

"You can't be a farmer when you wear a coat like that."

Bolster fingered his lapels. "It comes with the job."

"What is your job?"

"Things are happening fast now, kid. It's time for you to come with me. And don't try the Machu Picchu report again."

Cooper looked back into the barn.

"Don't let the coat fool you, kid," Bolster said. "Remember, I'm faster than you're ever going to be."

"I'm not going to work for Senator Wickham."

Bolster shook his head. "My joy overflows, kid. Look, I know you've got guts. You don't have to show me. There's not a whole lot of kids who would stick it out here like you have. Especially now that it's getting cold." He put his hands in his pockets and turned around, looking out over the farm as if he could see it all, even in the dark. Maybe he could.

Then he turned back. "So what's it to be?" Bolster leaned toward him. "You want to know more than anything in the world who's waiting for you, don't you, kid? You want to know so bad your hands are sweating— even in a cold like this. And the thing is, you've got the guts to come find out."

And suddenly, Cooper thought of what Mr. Searle had said: Something was going to happen that nobody had planned on.

He did want to know. And his hands were sweating.

Bolster took his keys out of his pocket. "Let's go," he said.

When Bolster walked out into the darkness and toward the jeep parked on the side of the house—the side away from Mrs. Perley's window—Cooper waited only a moment. He followed, hesitated, and then climbed in.

"You ever ridden in a jeep before?"

"No."

"Buckle up so you don't fall out."

"I'm not going to fall out."

Bolster looked at him. "Is everyone in New Hampshire as stubborn as you? Because I don't drive like Mrs. Perley. I've driven through swamps in Burma, across deserts in North Africa, and straight up mountains in Tibet."

"I drive a Farmall through a field so fast, the rows heat up. And when I'm done with that, I drive through cedars and take out mailboxes," said Cooper.

Bolster laughed out loud. "Kid, I always figured I would like you. But you still have to buckle up. The person who wants to meet you wouldn't be happy if you came in two pieces."

Bolster did drive fast—faster than a Farmall, faster than Old Ford, and a whole lot faster than Mrs. Perley's Plymouth. So fast that the wind whipped away any words. They geared out of Cooper's driveway, rushed past Mrs. Perley's house, blurred down Main and by New Lincoln Common, and careened south onto the highway toward Keene. In the dark, they passed the exits where most folks were safe in their beds. Cooper looked at them jealously. The lights gleaming in scattered houses seemed as far away as stars.

They rode on through the night like a meteor, and in the jeep, Cooper felt like there was hardly enough car between him and the road to keep him from flying out. He tried to imagine what it would be like to ride with Bolster across swamps and deserts and mountains, but then decided he'd best just hang on for now. He tried to do that while he hugged his coat around himself.

"Our exit, kid," shouted Bolster.

"Where are we going?"

But if Bolster could hear him, he made no sign of it, and when he took the exit, Cooper couldn't have listened to him anyway, since he was busy hanging on to the frame and hoping the seat belt wouldn't give out.

"You always take corners like that?"

"That's what corners are made for, kid."

Past a few farms—all dark—then past some outlying houses—mostly dark—and then into the town center—mostly lit up—and finally to a fancier hotel than Cooper had ever seen—all lit up.

Bolster swerved the jeep around back and jerked it to a stop.

"You're lucky you didn't get a ticket, going into town that fast."

"I don't get tickets, kid. I've driven through swamps in Burma, across deserts in North Africa, and—"

"Yeah, I know: straight up mountains in Taiwan."

"Tibet, kid. Straight up mountains in Tibet. Make sure you take Geography next semester. Now listen, don't talk to anyone until we get inside, understand? No one here is going to hurt you. But this isn't kid stuff you're into now. Someone who thinks he can take care of a whole dairy farm by himself should know what I'm talking about."

They climbed out of the jeep. Bolster came around, put his hand on Cooper's elbow, and guided him to the back of the hotel. A guard stood at the door as they came up, but he moved aside to let them in. More guards waited in the hallway as they passed the laundry, the kitchen, and the staff restrooms; each time the guards moved aside as they passed. At the end of the hall, a guard got on the elevator to ride up with them, and when the doors opened, six more guards checked the ID that Bolster was carrying. Three guards ahead and three behind, they walked down the hall and up a flight of stairs with carpet so thick their footsteps made no noise. Down another hall, then a waiting guard opened a door for them. The three guards ahead separated, and Cooper and Bolster went in. Bolster let go of his elbow for the first time since they'd left the jeep.

"Nice place, eh, kid?"

It was a nice place. He was sinking up to his ankles in the carpet now and seeing himself in mirrors that filled whole walls. Yellow flowers bloomed all over on tables with legs that seemed way too thin. The whole place smelled like a greenhouse.

"It could use some cows," said Cooper.

Bolster laughed. "The manure would be a problem. Give me your coat."

They waited in the heat of the room, Bolster standing silently, Cooper beside him. A clock ticked dully. The sound of a train whistle came from far away—a lonely sound.

Then a door by one of the mirrors opened without a sound, and a man in a pinstripe suit, perfectly dressed still this late at night, stepped in. He left the door behind him ajar.

Everything grew colder. Very much colder. Cooper wished he had his coat back.

"This him?" he said.

"Yes, sir."

Mr. Pinstripe nodded. He crossed the room to a desk

and, unlocking a lower drawer, took out a folder. He looked inside it, then looked at Cooper. "You've been giving us a whole lot of trouble." He looked down in the folder again. "Cooper Jewett. Age fourteen. Grandparents Eli and Edna Jewett. Parents deceased in a car crash." He looked up at Cooper, and Cooper stared back. Then he looked into the folder again. "Grandmother deceased. Grandfather deceased. Rural Route Number Three, New Lincoln, New Hampshire. Case File Number 0841494 in New Hampshire Social Services. Recommended for removal from present situation to the state foster-care system." He looked up. "Any mistakes so far?"

"Just the part about removal."

Mr. Pinstripe smiled. "Bolster said you've got guts. Do you?"

"When I need them."

Mr. Pinstripe considered. "A fair answer. You might need them now. You could have been taken off the farm days ago. Your farm should have been sold, along with the cows. The only reason this hasn't happened already is because of who's in the next room."

Cooper hoped it wasn't Mr. Pinstripe that he had come to meet. He hoped it was whoever was in the next room. He even let himself think, just for a moment, that maybe, maybe, maybe the person in the next room was his—

"We thought we could keep things quiet. We thought we could make it so you could stay on your farm. But we can't always have what we want. Especially when you're a day away from being the cause of one of the biggest scandals in American history."

"Mister, I don't know what you're talking about. I've never even been outside New Hampshire."

"No, you haven't. Not once, it says here. You met Senator Wickham, though."

"Yes."

"What did he want?"

"He asked me to be part of his campaign."

"What did you say?"

"No."

"Anything else?"

Cooper began to shiver, even in the heat of that room. He put his hands in his pockets and held his arms close to his sides.

"Did he ask you for any papers? Birth certificates, things like that?"

"Yes."

"Did you give him anything?"

"No. Your guys took those later."

Mr. Pinstripe was very still. "Our guys. They took what later?"

"You sent two guys to get my birth certificate, and my medical records—and to just about tear my arm off.

And I don't know what else you want, but I've got cows that need milking tomorrow morning, and I need to get up early to do it. So if you want me to tell Senator Wickham one more time that I'm not going to work for his campaign, let's get it over with."

Suddenly Mr. Pinstripe was right next to him, smaller than Bolster, but so fierce. "You better get control of yourself, Cooper, because the way I see it, one phone call from me and those cows of yours will be hamburger wrapped in cellophane tomorrow afternoon at the local supermarket. Now, Cooper, think. The pictures of you that Senator Wickham has—how did he get them?"

"He hid some cameras in the barn."

"When?"

"Some night a while ago. I tried to find them but never did. I guess they're still there."

A sudden indrawn breath from Bolster. Mr. Pinstripe looked at him, and Bolster nodded.

And Mr. Pinstripe said something that Cooper's grandfather would not have allowed—even in the barn.

"Why does it matter to you?" asked Cooper.

"It matters," Mr. Pinstripe said, "because right now, over at America for Wickham headquarters, they're developing glossy photographs of you and Bolster together, and then they'll start to plan the inaugural ball." He slapped the folder back onto the desk.

Cooper looked at Bolster, then back at Mr. Pinstripe. "You don't want the two of us seen together."

Mr. Pinstripe said nothing.

"You don't work for Senator Wickham," said Cooper.

"You're starting to figure things out," said Mr. Pinstripe. "Only it's a little late."

"So who do you both work for?"

But Mr. Pinstripe didn't have time to answer. Instead, a voice came from the next room. "They work for me."

And then the President of the United States walked in, and she held out her hand.

Cooper had imagined flying an F-14. He had imagined coming down out of the clouds onto the deck of the USS *Constellation*, Captain Perley commanding, and the feel of his wheels thunking onto the deck, the jerk of the wire grabbing the undercarriage, the thunder of his engines suddenly reversing as he landed on a little strip of safety in a sea of blue.

Cooper had imagined playing second base for the Boston Red Sox in the World Series. He had imagined the popcorn–hot dog–beer smell of the crowd mingling with the heady smell of the mown grass and the red dust of the infield, and the cheers when he came up in the bottom of the ninth, and the sweat of the pitcher who knew that here at the plate was the game winner and there wasn't a single thing he could do about it.

And most of all, and dearest of all—and the one dream that he tried not to let come too often because it seemed it could never be true—Cooper had imagined his parents walking up the driveway onto the farm, their hands held high in the air, waving, their eyes telling him everything he had longed to hear from them.

But in all his dreaming, he had never imagined that he would shake the hand of the President of the United States, in a warm hotel room filled with yellow flowers, on a cold starry night in New Hampshire.

"Cooper Jewett," she said. She took his hand and held it tightly. Then she put her other hand on his shoulder. "I've heard so much about you. I've wanted to meet you for a very long time." She smiled a wavery smile and led him over to one of the couches, where they sat down close beside each other. The President let go of his hand and brushed her hair back behind her ears— ears that stuck out farther than probably she wished they did.

They had sat down by the mirrors, and their reflections jumped from glass to glass, back and forth across the room. Whenever they moved, an infinite number of Coopers and Presidents moved with them.

"Ma'am—Mrs. President," said Cooper, "I can't believe I'm sitting here with you. I mean, the President of the United States."

She laughed lightly. "No, no, Cooper. I wondered if I

would ever see you. After all, a boy running a dairy farm on his own has to be just as busy as I am."

Cooper could hardly speak. He was sitting on a couch with the President of the United States. She still held his shoulder. She was looking at him as though she couldn't get enough of the sight.

"Madam President," began Mr. Pinstripe.

"Bolster says you're a runner," said the President.

"Bolster says that I'm a terrible runner."

She laughed again. "Bolster thinks everyone is a terrible runner unless he's won Nationals. But look at you—a little bigger than I thought, and stronger. With the shoulders of a boy who has done farm chores all his life. It looks like growing up in New Lincoln has been good for you."

"Madam President," said Mr. Pinstripe again.

She let go of Cooper's shoulder. "I know. We don't have much time." She looked back at Cooper. "Let me introduce you to the First Gentleman."

Then, as if he were putting on a play and had been cued, the First Gentleman came into the room, wearing a suit as formal as Mr. Pinstripe's but looking like he'd had enough of it for that day—sort of the way Cooper usually felt toward the end of services at New Lincoln Methodist. He was tall and thin, with a forehead set forward like he was about to holler.

"I hear you're quite the farmer," he said, and shook Cooper's hand too. His eyes moved up and down him.

"A lot of people seem to know a lot about me," Cooper said.

"Some would like to know more," said the President.

"There isn't all that much to know."

"I think there's a great deal to know," said the President. "A boy with no parents and no grandparents, all on his own. Running a dairy farm on his own."

"I have help," said Cooper. "Mrs. Perley up the hill and Mr. Searle down below."

The President nodded. "Good neighbors can mean a great deal. But they aren't parents, are they, Cooper?"

"I had grandparents."

"And what were they like?" asked the First Gentleman, sitting down. He joined the infinite number of Coopers and Presidents.

"Well, they didn't like politicians much."

The President laughed. "That's a good start. We don't like many politicians either."

"They loved each other," he said.

A pause. Then the President whispered, "And they loved you too, didn't they?"

*Of course they did,* thought Cooper to himself. But he didn't say anything. It wasn't something to talk about.

"Tell us what it was like, growing up on a farm," said the First Gentleman.

But Cooper knew he could never tell them what it was like to grow up on a farm. How could he explain to people who lived in rooms with yellow flowers and mirrors what he felt when he milked Moon and Star on a cold, cold morning, pressing himself against their soft, warm sides? How could he explain what it tasted like to eat cucumbers that had been growing a few minutes before supper in his grandmother's garden? How could he tell about the smell of the dark earth turned over in long furrows or the mica glinting on the rocks he lugged to the stone walls or the satisfying *thwack* of a hatchet and the twin halves of blond oak ready for the woodstove?

How could you explain all that to the President of the United States?

"It's all I've ever known," he said.

"Were you happy?" asked the President.

"Madam President," interrupted Mr. Pinstripe. "I've already advised against this. Bolster and I—"

But the President held up her hand, and Mr. Pinstripe stopped talking. The President's green eyes never left Cooper's.

"I hope you've been happy," she said. "I hope you haven't missed your parents, since you never really knew them. But I can promise you this: If they had

★ 130 ★

known you, and if they could have seen what a fine young man you've grown up to be, they would have been very, very proud. I know they would have." She took his hands again in her own. "So proud."

The broken part of Cooper twisted and curled deep inside him, and it was all he could do to keep it from moving into place again. The memory of its rhythms staggered him. They had come so close to starting again. He trembled.

Then he looked at the President's eyes—her beautiful green eyes—and he saw that she knew what had almost happened.

And he saw that she was almost glad.

And that she was very afraid.

He wanted to say to her, *Don't be afraid. Don't be afraid. I won't let it start again. I can never let it start again. Don't be afraid.*

But who was he to tell the President of the United States not to be afraid?

The memory of the rhythms grew fainter and fainter. Then they stopped. But his trembling did not.

"Madam President," said Mr. Pinstripe.

She looked over at him and took her hands away from Cooper. He realized that she had been trembling too. But after a moment she sighed, then looked back at Cooper. "There's always something to take you away from the thing you really want to be doing," she said.

"I think that running for re-election is something you really want to be doing," said Mr. Pinstripe. "And when you run for re-election, you have to give speeches. And when you have to give speeches—"

"You have to practice them," finished the President. "All right, Barrett, all right." She took Cooper's hand again. Then she looked in the mirror, and Cooper looked with her. They sat on the couch, an infinite number of them, and every one close together.

"Well, then," she said quietly. She and the First Gentleman stood. "We'll see you in the morning, Cooper." And then she was gone, Mr. Pinstripe—Barrett—with her.

★ ★ ★ ★ ★ ★ ★ ★ ★

# CHAPTER EIGHT

When the door shut behind the President, Cooper began to think not of the President or Bolster or the hothouse room with the yellow flowers. He thought of Mrs. Perley and Mr. Searle. He thought of the dining room breakfasts that Mrs. Perley made for the three of them. Of the milking that Mr. Searle did every morning and evening. He thought of the way that, sometimes, they would look at each other across the table. Like his grandparents had.

How had he not seen it before?

"You'll be staying with us for a few days," the First Gentleman said, "until things quiet down. Are you listening, son?"

*I should have seen it a long time ago,* thought Cooper.

"Just a few days."

Cooper looked at the First Gentleman through the moist haze of the room. "I'm sorry," he said, "I'm going home."

"You haven't been listening, Cooper. You're not going home. You'll be with us for a few days."

"No," said Cooper, shaking his head. "I'm going home."

The First Gentleman laughed. "No? No? Do you know how many people in the world would crawl across the country on their knees to meet with the President of the United States in the morning?"

"They don't have dairy cows."

The First Gentleman laughed again. "You were right about him, Bolster. Dead on. Cooper, you're just like I was when I was your age. So stubborn you wouldn't take the sun if someone offered it, because you wanted the moon instead. But sometimes, you take what you're given. I think Mr. Barrett told you why you were here."

"I'm about to cause the biggest scandal in American history, even though I've never been out of New Hampshire."

"Something like that. There's someone who wants to use you to destroy the President's chances of re-election."

"Senator Wickham."

The First Gentleman nodded slowly. "That's right, Cooper. And to do that, Senator Wickham will lie to make the President seem . . . to make the President quit the race."

"Then show that he's lying."

The First Gentleman looked at Bolster and smiled. "You don't live in the world we live in, Cooper. It doesn't matter if it's a lie or not—once it airs on the six o'clock news, it's truth, and no amount of denying changes it."

"Maybe things would be okay if I just stayed where I was, and everyone left me alone."

"Maybe," said the First Gentleman slowly. "But I can't play with maybes. It could be that you'd just go on back to Lincolnville—"

"New Lincoln."

"But it could be too that things wouldn't be okay. We need to be sure." He leaned back into the couch. "There's a cabin up in New Brunswick. Ever been up there? I haven't in years. Nice place, all alone on a lake with decent-sized trout. Some steelheads. It's too cold to swim in, but you'll never find better fishing anywhere. Right, Bolster?"

"Not anywhere, sir."

Cooper looked at Bolster, whose face didn't show a thing.

"The President wants to see you tomorrow morning," the First Gentleman said. "After that, we'll have some people take you up there."

"For how long?"

"Cheer up, Cooper. A few weeks away from school. Fishing all day long. I would have given anything if I could have had that when I was fourteen. And if you're anything like me—and you are—you'll have a great time. Think of it as a mid-year vacation."

Cooper imagined Mr. Searle at morning milking, waiting for him and finally coming up to the house, where Mrs. Perley would be frantic because she couldn't find him. He thought of his farm, quiet now in the dark—the cows waking up, the early light on the land. And he thought of his grandfather.

*You're my first boy, Cooper, my first boy.*

"I guess I'm not," Cooper said.

"Not what?" said the First Gentleman.

"Not anything like you."

The First Gentleman's face hardened. He stood, and his brow leaned forward. Bolster coughed slightly and shook his head at Cooper—just a bit.

"There was a letter that was sent with the medical files and the birth certificate," the First Gentleman said. "Have you seen that letter?"

"No."

"You sure?"

"I'm sure."

"It's important that we find it." He paused. "Very important."

"It's important that I get home for morning milking," said Cooper. He leaned forward. "Very important."

"Don't be smart, kid," said Bolster. "There's a lot more going on here than you know about. Tell us where the letter is."

"Is that what the President wants to see me about in the morning?"

"One of the reasons," said the First Gentleman.

"Then she'll be disappointed," he said.

The First Gentleman crossed the room to the desk and picked up the folder that Mr. Pinstripe had slapped onto it. "Case Number 0841494," he read aloud. "That's you, Cooper. You're a fourteen-year-old boy who is just a number. And you're about to lose everything. The farm, the cows, everything. All you need to do is to cooperate, Cooper. Just cooperate. And then we can make this whole file go away. Someday, you can go back to your farm, and no one will bother you again."

The First Gentleman put the folder back on the desk.

"Cooper, you're all alone in the world. Make the right decision."

Cooper stared at the First Gentleman. "I'll make do," he said quietly.

The First Gentleman took the folder and walked around the desk. He opened a lower drawer and put it in. He looked up at Cooper. "You'll make do," he said. He shut the drawer and locked it. "Enjoy the trout,

Cooper. They fight like mad, but after a while, they always give in." And the First Gentleman left the room.

Bolster sighed. "Kid, you do know who you're talking to, right? This is the President and First Gentleman of the United States. It's not Joe Farmer from down the dirt road a piece."

"I know who they are," said Cooper.

"Then you should tell him where the letter is."

"Suppose I said that my grandmother burned it up? Could I go home then?"

Bolster shook his head. "It's like the First Gentleman said: You don't always get what you want. Take your coat and let's go."

At the door, Bolster put his hand on Cooper's elbow again and led him into the group of six guards who were still standing outside. They walked with them back to the elevator and waited wordlessly until Cooper and Bolster stepped inside.

"Real friendly," said Cooper when the doors closed.

"Yeah," said Bolster. "We're known for hospitality."

Down two stories and then out into another hall with a carpet not as thick as the one they had left and only two guards waiting for them. They walked to the very end of the hall, Bolster's hand still on Cooper's elbow, down another hall, and then another, until they reached a room with an open door.

"This door locks from the outside," Bolster said,

pushing him lightly in. "I don't want you to disappoint the President. When I come to get you in the morning, try to remember who you're talking to." He closed the door, and Cooper heard the lock click. When he tried the doorknob, it didn't move.

There wasn't much in the room: a couple of beds, a chair upholstered with dark yellow flowers, and a table with a vase full of dark yellow flowers that scented the air. They were the same dark yellow as the lampshades and the bedspreads and the curtains and the wallpaper and the towels by the bathroom sink and the bathroom sink itself. All dark yellow.

He parted the curtains and looked out the window. He was only three stories up, but none of the buildings here at the back of the hotel were any higher, and since there weren't many lights this late at night, he could see far out over the town, tracing its rows of streetlights in the darkness. Beyond, only a few lights glimmered here and there, as though some of the night stars had fallen down and were bent a little but still trying to twinkle despite it all. Cooper opened the window, and the cold of New Hampshire came into the heated room. He put on his coat and breathed in the air like it had just come down from the Near Pasture.

Then he looked back at the beds.

Cooper had seen old black-and-white movies where the hero tied sheets together to escape. He had always figured it was a gag. But there were two beds in the room, and the room was only on the third floor, and if he tied all four sheets together, they'd probably reach the ground.

He looked out the window again. The air was crisp in his lungs.

He decided to try.

He ripped the sheets off the beds, knotted them all together, and tied one end around the bedpost. He pulled, and the bed didn't move. Then he went back to the window, looked out to see if there were any guards walking down below, and threw the bundle of sheets outside. They didn't quite reach the ground—but it wouldn't be a long drop. Turning the lights out in his room, he tugged hard three or four times again to be sure the sheets wouldn't give, climbed out onto the sill, and lowered himself into the night.

He looked up, expecting to see Bolster appear at the window to haul him in.

He looked down, expecting six guards to holler.

But no one hauled him in, and no one hollered.

So hand after hand, hand after hand, he clambered down the sheets. He climbed past some ledges and past some darkened windows, trying not to kick against anything, trying not to make any noise at all. When he reached the bottom of the sheets, he was swaying back and forth, but he wasn't too high. He let himself down as far as he could go, and timing the sway, he leaped onto the grass.

No one had seen him.

No one except Mrs. Perley and Mr. Searle, who drove up beside him in Mrs. Perley's Plymouth.

Cooper stood as stunned as if someone had just handed him the moon.

"Get in!" cried Mr. Searle, opening the rear door.

Cooper did, and he jerked back against the seat when Mrs. Perley hit the accelerator harder than she had ever hit it before in her whole life. "Gracious goodness," she said. "Whatever would Edna say?"

Mrs. Perley, Mr. Searle, and Cooper sped along the interstate toward New Lincoln, faster than Cooper had ever thought Mrs. Perley's Plymouth could go.

"Sarah Perley," said Mr. Searle, "the speed limit on this highway is sixty-five miles per hour. Not eighty-five miles per hour. Sixty-five miles per hour."

"Are you driving, you old coot?"

"We'll either have a ticket or a wreck, one."

"The answer to my question is, 'No, I am not driving, Mrs. Perley, so I should leave it entirely in your able hands—which have never, ever come close to even scratching this beautiful car.'"

"You're at ninety!"

"You read extremely well for someone of your advanced age." She looked back at Cooper. "Are you all right?"

"At least watch the dang road," said Mr. Searle.

"I'm all right," said Cooper.

"Obscenity is not called for," said Mrs. Perley.

"Tying sheets together to climb out the window. Thought they only did that in the movies," said Mr. Searle.

"So did I. I'm just glad I wasn't on the top floor. How did you find me?"

"You can thank the old grump for that," said Mrs. Perley. "He looked out his window and saw brake lights on your place where there should not be brake lights. By the time he came up, you were just pulling out. He woke me and told me to get into his pickup, because we were going to see what there was to see. A suggestion was made about returning the favor of a bloodied nose." She looked at Mr. Searle. "Ha!" she said.

"Watch the road, Sarah Perley. You've never gone this fast in all your life."

Cooper looked at the speedometer. It read ninety-two.

"Of course, I would never sit in an old pickup that has been washed neither inside nor out since before the Flood."

"So," said Mr. Searle, "we had to get into her Plymouth—that starts only when it has a mind to."

"It only gives trouble when cantankerous people sit in it," said Mrs. Perley.

"Funny it ever starts at all, then."

Mrs. Perley glared at him.

"By the time we got through New Lincoln," said Mr. Searle, "we'd broke every speed limit in the county."

"So you followed us," said Cooper.

"I tell you," said Mrs. Perley, "it was easy. Did you know he was only going seventy-five miles per hour? I do not know why it took me so very long to see the pleasure in rapid driving."

"We saw you go into the hotel," said Mr. Searle, "and we drove around town looking for three open parking spaces together so Mario Andretti here could pull in without another car next to her."

"There is not enough parking in that town," said Mrs. Perley.

"So we've been driving around all this time, trying not to look suspicious. And then we saw you climbing down sheets like Errol Flynn," said Mr. Searle. "Isn't responsible for a New Hampshire dairyman, acting like a movie star, you know."

"I know," said Cooper.

They drove out of town and into the dark of the

countryside, and Cooper told them who he had met, and Mrs. Perley said "Oh, my gracious goodness" and Mr. Searle sniffed "Well, she's only a Democrat." Cooper sat back, listening to them fuss at each other, and felt again the strong tightening of what was broken in him. It came upon him sudden and surprising. He wasn't sure what to do with it. And he wasn't sure he could hold it down much longer.

Mr. Searle fussed at Mrs. Perley the rest of the way home, but she didn't care. She stayed around ninety the whole way, took the New Lincoln exit at a brisk fifty-five, and stayed around sixty as they passed New Lincoln Common.

"Never have seen it this closed down before," said Mr. Searle.

"That is because you have never been up this late before," said Mrs. Perley.

"No respectable dairyman is," said Mr. Searle. "Where to take the boy? Your house or mine?"

"Mine," said Cooper.

"Do you think that is safe?" said Mrs. Perley. "It does seem that lately anyone at all might appear on your kitchen porch."

"It's late now," said Mr. Searle. "No one else in the whole world is up. I expect he'll be fine."

"And I've got the milking tomorrow morning—but I guess it already is tomorrow morning."

They took the hill down toward Cooper's farm. The sky was already more a deep purple than a black, and Cooper wondered if he should bother going to sleep at all.

"There is a red light behind us," said Mrs. Perley.

Cooper looked around. The red light flashed some distance back.

Mrs. Perley turned to Mr. Searle. "No one else in the whole world is up?"

"Might be a state trooper, the way you've been tearing down these roads," said Mr. Searle.

"I wouldn't be surprised if it was the czar of all the Russians come to call on Cooper," said Mrs. Perley.

"Whoever it is, they're coming closer," said Cooper. The red lights seemed to flash even faster.

"You know the old Lime Kiln Road?" asked Mr. Searle.

"Of course I know the old Lime Kiln Road," said Mrs. Perley. "I have lived here all my life. Do I know the old Lime Kiln Road."

"Take it."

"I am not going to take the old Lime Kiln Road. Nobody has driven on the old Lime Kiln Road since you were a boy, you old goat. Do you have any idea what that road would do to my car?"

"Some idea," said Mr. Searle. "You have any idea who might be in that car and what they might want with Cooper here?"

"Some idea," said Mrs. Perley quietly.

Mr. Searle nodded.

"The flashing light's closer," said Cooper.

They went past the Jewett farm, up a hill, and around a long bend in the road. Then, with a sigh and a jerk of the wheel, Mrs. Perley took a sharp, unexpected right onto the old Lime Kiln Road. At the first hard thunk she groaned. At the second she groaned again. At the third she reached over and smacked Mr. Searle.

"What's that for?"

"It is to make me feel better, you old noodle."

She slowed as they took a sharp downhill. She slowed even more when they took a sharp uphill. With every turn of the wheels, gravel clattered and smattered against the underside of the Plymouth. Looking at her reflection in the rearview mirror, Cooper saw Mrs. Perley grimace.

The trees began to thicken and lean closer in to the road, and Mrs. Perley drove slower and slower, until suddenly her headlights hit the old lime kiln itself, squatting on the edge of a deep ravine. It was hidden by birch saplings that had grown up around it, but Cooper could still make it out. It seemed ancient and out of place, like a dinosaur that had hibernated here away from the years.

"This is where the road ends," said Mrs. Perley.

She turned the headlights off, and they got out. In the quiet and cold dark of the night, they stood together, the three of them.

And then they saw the red lights flashing up the gravel road.

Mr. Searle took Cooper by the shoulders. "Good dairyman always knows his directions," he said.

Cooper nodded.

"Good dairyman always keeps his head on his shoulders so he knows what he has to do and how he has to do it."

Cooper nodded again.

"South of here is the old Croft place. You know it?" Cooper nodded. "The road that heads out from there goes west. When it turns sharp north, keep on into the woods a quarter mile. Those are the trees above the Hurd place. Go."

"Why the Hurd place?"

"Because they love you too," said Mrs. Perley.

Cooper looked at her.

And then Cooper felt whatever it was that had broken in him when his grandfather had died shift hugely, then spring back into place and begin its rhythms once again. Cooper had no idea how it had happened, but he knew that it had happened. The tears that sprang to the edges of his eyes were tears of a sorrowing gladness, and he did not know whether to laugh out loud or fall into Mrs. Perley's arms.

"Go," said Mr. Searle again.

Cooper felt the rhythms growing stronger and stronger.

Lord, stronger than the sorrow. He took Mr. Searle's warm hand. He kissed Mrs. Perley's warm cheek.

"Go," said Mrs. Perley.

And then the flashing lights were close.

Cooper went. He climbed up and above the lime kiln, its old chalky smell still dusting the air. He clambered onto the granite ledge that leveled off past the kiln and pushed into the cedars that had taken root in the dark rock.

But he was hardly into them before he looked back and saw the flashing lights throwing an eerie red onto the lime kiln below, as though it were once again on fire and burning marble into ash.

Cooper heard a car skid against the gravel. Heard a car door open and close. Footsteps. Heard the voice of Sheriff Gibbs.

"You folks figuring on burning for some lime?" he said.

"Yes," came the voice of Mr. Searle.

"And you do that at night, do you?"

"You've caught us, Sheriff," said Mrs. Perley. "Mr. Searle and I are out here to perform incantations against troublesome sheriffs, calling down upon them flat tires and broken jail cells and all manner of trial and tribulation."

"I'm almost ready to believe that, Mrs. Perley. You folks been anywhere else tonight?"

"Drag racing," said Mr. Searle.

"I'm almost ready to believe that too. I've got a report up from Keene here. Report about a blue Plymouth. Sort of like yours, Mrs. Perley. Speeding something awful. Something about the Jewett boy. You haven't seen him, have you?"

"What would Cooper be doing on the old Lime Kiln Road?" she said.

"Hard to tell. Then again, it's hard to tell what you two are doing out here. I'd investigate the speeding charge—hard as it is to believe, Mrs. Perley. But it's the Jewett boy I'm looking for. Any idea where he might be?"

"I suppose sound asleep in his bed," said Mrs. Perley, and Cooper wondered if that was the first straight-out lie that Mrs. Perley had ever told.

"No, he's not there. But I think you both already know that."

"Knowing is a whole lot different from telling," said Mr. Searle.

"It's best to cooperate, folks. There's more here than one kid."

"Raymond Gibbs," said Mrs. Perley, "that 'one kid,' as you say, is worth more to me than most anything else."

Cooper heard another car grind against the gravel as it drove up. Another door opened, then closed. Footsteps. Slower.

"Sheriff," Mr. Searle said, "that's one of the men who attacked me in my own house."

"I know," said Sheriff Gibbs. "Why don't you tell us where the boy is, and he won't attack you again."

Cooper crept out of the cedars and back onto the granite ledge. Looking down over the kiln, he could see Mr. Searle and Mrs. Perley, standing side by side, and maybe—it was hard to tell since they stood out of the headlights—they were holding hands. Standing smack in the middle of the headlights shining from a black sedan were the sheriff and a Very Big Man.

As quietly as he could, Cooper shinnied down the side of the kiln.

"Where's the boy?" asked Sheriff Gibbs again.

At the bottom of the kiln, Cooper snuck along the edge of the old Lime Kiln Road, keeping low within the brush. He saw the Very Big Man look his way, but just for a moment.

"He's a dairyman," said Mr. Searle. "He's home in bed this time of night."

Cooper came out onto the road behind the sheriff's patrol car.

"You're a dairyman, and you're not home in bed," said the sheriff. "And it seems you're not a very quick learner." The Very Big Man moved closer.

Cooper quietly opened the sheriff's door and got in.

He found the key in the ignition and looked around for the clutch.

"You will never get another vote in this county," said Mrs. Perley.

Cooper realized that the patrol car was going to be more complicated than the Farmall.

"By the time this is over, I'll be a bureau chief in Washington, D.C.," said Sheriff Gibbs.

Cooper gave up on the clutch. He turned the key and ripped the patrol car into gear.

Then three things happened.

The car careened forward, and Sheriff Gibbs and the Very Big Man leaped off the old Lime Kiln Road into the woods, their yells louder than the roar of the engine—which, Cooper noticed, was missing some.

Second, Mr. Searle spun Mrs. Perley away from her car.

And third, the patrol car jerked to a halt on the gravel when Cooper stomped on the brake, but it still skidded into Mrs. Perley's blue Plymouth, nudging it just enough to tip the Plymouth toward the ravine. It balanced on the edge. Then its back end looked up at the stars for a moment, hesitated, and disappeared. The sound of the front end shattering on the rocks below came soon enough.

"Oh," said Mr. Searle.

"My Plymouth," said Mrs. Perley.

"Get in!" hollered Cooper.

Mr. Searle pushed her into the front seat of the patrol car and got in next to her.

"There's no clutch," said Cooper.

"My Plymouth," said Mrs. Perley.

Mr. Searle looked behind them. The sheriff and the Very Big Man were back on the road, and there was no room for the patrol car to turn around. "Go," he said.

Cooper pushed into reverse and hit the accelerator. Somehow the red lights and the siren came on too, and Cooper was speeding backward, past the black sedan, and past the sheriff and the Very Big Man—who were leaping into the woods again. Gravel flew everywhere.

"My Plymouth," said Mrs. Perley.

And Mr. Searle started to laugh. "You see them jump into the woods?"

And Cooper began to laugh too, thinking of how he had almost clipped the sheriff's big . . . well, thinking of how he had almost clipped the sheriff.

And then the old Lime Kiln Road turned as it went down the hill, and Cooper got confused going in reverse and fishtailed off the road.

They all sat breathing heavily. The siren hollered, and the red lights glared against the trees.

"You did not run down any mailboxes," pointed out Mrs. Perley.

"But there's probably a whole row of cedars gone," said Mr. Searle.

And then the sheriff and the Very Big Man ran down to each side of the car.

The sheriff couldn't speak, he was so out of breath. And he was mad too—so mad his considerable chin was wobbling. Cooper wasn't sure if it was only the lights that were making his face so red.

The Very Big Man pulled open the door by Mr. Searle and reached in for him.

"No," said Mr. Searle, and he tried to pull the door closed.

But the Very Big Man held it open easily. He grabbed Mr. Searle's shoulder.

"All of you, get out," said Sheriff Gibbs. "Now. You don't want to see what my associate will do if any of you are still in there in five seconds."

But they never did find out what it was the Very Big Man was going to do.

★ ★ ★ ★ ★ ★ ★ ★ ★ ★

# CHAPTER NINE

THERE WAS A THUNK, and the Very Big Man's head hit the roof of the patrol car. He went slack and slumped down past Mr. Searle, a startled look on his Very Big face.

"Who in blue blazes are—" began the sheriff, but he didn't finish. He flew back from the patrol car and lay moaning on the side of the old Lime Kiln Road, with something considerable sticking up into the air.

The door by Cooper opened. Bolster reached in and turned off the siren and flashing lights.

"You know, kid, only people in old movies use sheets to escape from hotels."

"I didn't have a hang glider."

"That would be style." Bolster got in and crammed Cooper against Mrs. Perley and Mr. Searle. "Kid, you sure do have guts," he said, and curled the car back onto the road, taking care to miss the sheriff and the Very Big Man. He started slowly out.

"How did you find us?"

"It's almost five o'clock in the morning, and I'm driving out of New Lincoln and down to the Jewett farm. Then I see red lights and hear sirens way off in the woods. Somehow it made me think of you."

"Listen, I don't have anything to do with any scandal."

"Kid, it's not your fault, but, yes, you do."

"Who exactly are you?" asked Mrs. Perley.

"My name is Bolster, ma'am."

She leaned forward. "Does Mr. Bolster have a first name?"

"Eustachius Bolster."

"You-stay-shuss?" said Cooper.

"Shut up, kid."

Bolster drew the patrol car around, and headed down the old Lime Kiln Road.

"I'm not going back with you," said Cooper.

"Yeah," said Bolster. "I can see that you had everything under control. Kid, I don't know how much you know. But you're not safe here. It's not your fault, and it's not right, but it's still true. You're not safe. And—not meaning any disrespect, ma'am—Mrs. Perley and Mr. Searle here aren't going to be able to handle what's coming."

"What is coming, Eustachius?" asked Mrs. Perley.

Bolster came up to the top of the hill and slowed.

"That," said Bolster.

At the end of the old Lime Kiln Road, five black sedans waited, blocking them. The doors of the front sedan opened, and four men got out, among them Senator Wickham. Bolster stopped the patrol car and got out too.

"Morning, folks," said Senator Wickham.

"You're in my way, Senator," said Bolster.

"Yes."

"And it looks like one of your goons is sitting in my jeep."

"Yes," said Senator Wickham.

"The only people who sit in my jeep are ones I've invited to sit in my jeep."

"It doesn't matter," said Senator Wickham. "Your jeep apparently is not running. I suspect it won't be running for some time. I'm here about this young man."

"I know what you're here for. You're not taking him anywhere."

Senator Wickham smiled. He motioned to the other sedans, and Very Big Men poured out of them. "Yes, I am, Mr. Bolster. Call me an agent of the State of New Hampshire, to whose social services I will turn him over as soon as we've concluded our business. He's to be the star attraction at a press conference in Keene in a few hours. You're all welcome to come. I suspect that the President herself will be listening in."

The Very Big Men surrounded the patrol car and pulled open the doors.

Cooper saw two things on the old Lime Kiln Road as the Very Big Men dragged him toward a sedan. First, he saw eight Very Big Men pin Bolster against the sheriff's patrol car—that's how many it took. Second, he saw Sheriff Gibbs run up, still all out of breath, and Mrs. Perley smack him on his considerable chin.

The black sedans traveled in a pack down Route 10 and into Keene. They traveled slowly, tightly, protecting the sedan in the center, in which sat Cooper—alone. The doors were all locked from the front. Impenetrable glass separated him from the Very Big Man who was driving.

Cooper sat with his knees hunched up.

Which is the same way he sat several hours later on a folding chair in a dreary room in Senator Wickham's dreary campaign headquarters in Keene. On the walls was an America for Wickham poster, one corner rolled up and torn. Shredded paper and scattered Styrofoam cups littered the floor, so that it looked as if a light snow had come down through the ceiling the night before. There were no windows. It was cold. A television was on with the sound off.

Cooper looked at his grandfather's watch. Nine-thirty. He had been up all night, and he couldn't help but yawn. He hoped Bolster had gotten Mrs. Perley and Mr. Searle off the old Lime Kiln Road. He hoped Mrs. Perley hadn't tried to smack one of the Very Big Men. He hoped Mr. Searle had gotten his cows milked and herded out to the Far Pasture.

And he hoped all three of them were somewhere nearby right now.

He glanced down at his grandfather's watch again. At New Lincoln High School, Mr. Hupfer was starting World Cultures. He was probably looking at Cooper's empty seat and figuring that he was running around "experiencing" instead of reading books.

Then the door clicked open, and Senator Wickham came in holding two doughnuts and a cup of coffee. "Farmer like yourself will be wanting your morning poison. How do you take it?"

"Black," said Cooper. Senator Wickham handed him the coffee and a doughnut. Cooper sipped at the cup. He hated coffee his grandmother hadn't made.

"Hot enough?" said Senator Wickham.

Cooper took a bite from his doughnut.

"Cooper, understand I'm running a campaign here, and it's not for county sheriff. This is for the presidency of the United States."

"And you're willing to kidnap someone to get it."

"I'm not kidnapping anyone. I'm giving you a choice, Case Number 0841494. Yes, I know the case number too—even if it was restricted. If you help me, I can help you. But if not, Case Number 0841494, I'll hand you over to New Hampshire Social Services, and you'll lose everything."

"Kidnapping," said Cooper.

Senator Wickham shrugged. "In my business, a word means what you want it to mean. Besides, it wasn't me you were escaping from last night, was it? Do you think the President of the United States routinely invites farm boys from New Hampshire over for a chat? If I hadn't gotten to you, you would have disappeared for a good long while."

"But that's not what you want, is it?"

"No, it isn't. I want to do whatever it takes to have the truth come out."

"Like beating up Mr. Searle."

"Whatever it takes." Senator Wickham walked over to the TV and watched its silence. He took a bite from his doughnut. "We wear bare knuckles in campaigns, Cooper. Sometimes they get bloody." He turned and smiled. "I never did understand how someone could like coffee black."

Senator Wickham looked around and found another folding chair leaning against the wall. He put the rest of the doughnut in his mouth, took the chair, and sat close to Cooper. "You still don't have a clue who you are, do you? All that's gone on, and you still don't have a clue. I thought you were brighter than that." Senator Wickham looked at his watch. "Maybe it would be better for the cameras if you knew." He leaned so far forward that Cooper could smell him. Crumbs of doughnut hung on to the sides of his mouth.

"Fourteen years ago, a Mr. and Mrs. Hugh Bradford checked into a hospital in this very town of Keene. They had a son, and they named him Cooper. Cooper Bradford. An unusual name, don't you think? They paid in cash and left the hospital after three days with Baby Cooper's medical report and birth certificate. Very soon after that, all of Baby Cooper's records disappeared from the hospital. And they disappeared from county records. All of them. It was as if Baby Cooper had never been born. You can see that the couple in question was . . . influential, shall we say, in certain circles."

Cooper felt the coffee in his stomach turning kind of sour. He decided he'd better not drink any more.

"Soon after the Bradfords left the hospital, a baby was delivered to the home of Eli and Edna Jewett of New Lincoln, New Hampshire. The story went about that he was a relative, perhaps a grandnephew, or even a grandson, and that his parents had been killed in a car accident. There was no one left to raise him besides the Jewetts. The story gained credibility when it was repeated by the saintly Reverend and Mrs. Hurd of New Lincoln Methodist Church and by Captain and Mrs. Perley and by the industrious Mr. Searle. But not everyone in New Lincoln believed the story."

Cooper didn't say anything.

"Three years ago, certain . . . constituents . . . in New Hampshire heard about the mysterious Cooper Jewett, and despite several, shall we say, federal impediments, they began to trace the equally mysterious Mr. and Mrs. Hugh Bradford. They were surprised to find a great many rather surprising correspondences with another couple, a very ambitious couple, a very prominent couple, who were rumored to have had the misfortune to find themselves expecting a child while they were still unmarried—an embarrassment, since their wedding was to be as publicly political an event as every other part of their ambitious lives. It was then that Mr. and Mrs. Hugh Bradford decided to travel north, accompanied by the supposed Mrs. Hugh Bradford's secretary, who drove a jeep back then too."

Senator Wickham stood up. "At the news conference in"—he looked at his watch again—"ten minutes, you'll meet the doctor who delivered you, Cooper. And the nurses who were there with your mother. And maybe you won't be surprised when every one of them positively identifies Mr. and Mrs. Hugh Bradford as the First

Gentleman and President." He leaned over. "Cooper, you're the First Boy of the United States of America."

And Cooper threw the rest of his coffee onto Senator Wickham's bright white shirt.

Senator Wickham jerked back. He sputtered some words that senators shouldn't sputter. He raised his fist, and Cooper jumped out of his chair.

Senator Wickham stopped and smiled again. He looked around and picked up a napkin from the floor. "You know, Cooper, it doesn't matter to me what happens to you after this," he said, wiping his shirt. "So you choose. You could sit up on that stage quietly as we tell the world who your parents are. Or you could run away. The door's open, and I hear you're good at escaping. But if you run away, there won't be much of your old life left. No more cows and no more barns."

"You don't need me to sit up on the stage, if you think you've got proof."

"You're wrong, Cooper. A picture is worth everything. And you standing up there, with your ears out just like the President's—that will make every front page in America." He finished wiping at his shirt. "Cooper, you're the nomination. A President who abandons a child, she'll withdraw from the race before the six o'clock news even thinks of beginning." He took a comb out of his jacket pocket and tossed it to Cooper. "Don't look so glum. In a few minutes, yours will be the most famous face in America. And, Cooper"—he laughed—"I'm giving you back your parents. You should be thanking me."

He left. No lock clicked behind him.

Cooper threw his doughnut against the door and broke the comb in two. He paced around the room. If he could have seen himself from above, he would have thought he looked like a trapped animal.

Had his parents really given him away?

Was he the President's son?

Had they really just given him away?

Was he the First Boy?

Had they really, truly just given him away?

And then he knew! He stopped pacing.

He was the first boy—for his grandfather and his grandmother.

And then, as if they had both walked into the room, he felt them with him. He felt their old, hardened hands on his shoulders and smelled their sweet, milky scent. He could almost see them. He could almost hear them breathing.

He could feel his grandfather's hand tousle his hair.

He was their first boy. Their first boy.

And where the broken part had been, he now felt the deep rhythms.

On the silent television, the screen flicked to an image of the President and First Gentleman coming up to a podium, looking stricken. Cameras flashed like fireworks. The President held up her hand and nodded her head toward a microphone, while the First Gentleman stood off to the side, his eyes lovingly upon her. She looked as if Very Big Men had taken her dearest pet. And she looked mad enough to rip out their hearts.

Cooper turned the sound on.

". . . understand that Senator Wickham will be making an outrageous charge: that the First Gentleman and I are the parents of a child abandoned fourteen years ago. We stand before America today to deny the charge and to denounce Senator Wickham for bringing his campaign to a new low. Is there no shame that will curb his ambition? If he can think of nothing else, he should think of this innocent boy about to be thrown into a maelstrom of attention that he has never anticipated and which he does not deserve. A boy whose loss of both parents and grandparents has left him vulnerable to ludicrous claims such as this one. Has the Senator no honor? Has the Senator no decency?"

But in the cold, bare room, littered with shredded paper and Styrofoam cups, Cooper was no longer listening. He was looking at the way the First Gentleman's nose pugged up a bit at the end and how the President's ears stuck out, and thinking they both looked very familiar.

And he began to wonder for the very first time—for the very first time—if maybe, deep down, he wanted it to be true. The President's son. Living in the White House. Black sedans. Hannah Joyce reporting about him.

And most amazing of all, a mother and a father. Not grandparents, not neighbors. A mother and a father. For a moment he thought of standing between them, holding their hands. The moment was so sweet that it was more like a memory than a dream.

But then the next moment came, and he realized it was a dream.

And he realized too that it wasn't his dream.

The sweetness drifted away, leaving only the old familiar ache. And it wasn't visions of the White House and Hannah Joyce reporting live that soothed him. It was visions of his farm, the meadows, the cows, the barns. And, he realized, visions of Mrs. Perley. And Mr. Searle.

Then he knew that he no longer wanted it to be true. All he wanted was to be sitting in Mr. Hupfer's World Cultures class, the smell of fresh milk on his hands, a driver's license in his back pocket (he could still dream a little), and one of Mrs. Perley's raspberry tarts—well, maybe two, maybe three—waiting for him on the kitchen table when he got home.

All he wanted was home.

When the door clicked open again, Senator Wickham

came in, wearing a new white shirt and holding the folder marked *Cooper Jewett*. A Very Big Man came in behind him. "It's time," Senator Wickham said.

Cooper could tell the press conference was going to be a crowd long before he got there—the roiling waves of voices filled the hotel hallway, louder than the echoes of Senator Wickham's hard heels against the floor. And when they got to the door, Cooper saw he was right. The room was filled with more human beings than his pantry was filled with Mason jars. Maybe, if everyone exhaled, they could have gotten a few more reporters in. But there would have had to be a lot of squeezing before that happened.

Senator Wickham walked in first, and when he entered, the waves of voices lowered. When Cooper came in, propelled by a shove from the Very Big Man, the waves died down completely, and even with all those people crushed together, it was as silent as nightfall.

Senator Wickham put his hand on Cooper's shoulder and escorted him across the platform. He sat Cooper down on the folding chair that waited for him. The Very Big Man stood behind him. "Sit still, and you might keep your farm," whispered Senator Wickham.

Then he went to the podium.

"Ladies and gentlemen of the press," he began.

A bright light flashed, and instantly reporters stood

with their hands in the air, and there was such a shouting that Senator Wickham could hardly be heard.

Every hand pointed at Cooper.

"Is this the boy?"

"Any response to the President's charges this morning, Senator Wickham?"

"Senator, how did you find him?"

"Please, everyone," shouted the Senator, holding up his hand. "No need to shout. Everything in its time. I want to introduce to you this morning"—he paused and pointed toward Cooper, and everyone in the room went silent again—"Cooper Jewett."

"Are you the First Boy?" called out a reporter.

"Where have they been hiding you all these years?"

"Have you been meeting with your parents secretly?"

"Please, I know this is an amazing revelation, and there's no need for suspenseful melodramatics," said Senator Wickham. "Cooper Jewett has been positively identified as the child born to Mr. and Mrs. Hugh Bradford in Keene, fourteen years ago. And I am here to report to you today that Mr. and Mrs. Hugh Bradford have been positively identified as the President and First Gentleman of the United States. Cooper is the President's son, abandoned almost immediately after his birth by the President and First Gentleman in order to maintain their political ambitions untainted. They sacrificed their boy in the hope of a presidency. As you know, they were successful."

Lights dazzled Cooper as a thousand flashes went off at once.

Senator Wickham held up his hand. "This morning, the President, in yet another effort to salvage her political ambitions, accused me of lacking decency and honor. She accused me of dragging an innocent boy into a political fight. Perhaps a person who has abandoned a child should not use the words *decency* and *honor.* They would rather that the boy simply disappear 'for his own good,' she claims."

More hands raised up. More calls and lights flashing.

Cooper thought he might be sick.

Senator Wickham went on. "For his own good. As if a child who has no one, who is completely alone now that his alleged grandparents have passed on, who has been on his own for months now, with the President's full knowledge, can simply disappear, and that would be for his own good. As if a child can live without any expectation that his own parents might care for him, and that would be for his own good. This is the President whose policies on the American family we are urged to follow."

A reporter called out, "But if the President refuses to allow a DNA test, what proof do you have of these allegations?"

"It is awfully convenient that the President of the United States may refuse such tests while she is in office," said Senator Wickham. "Awfully convenient. Perhaps a President who has sworn that she is on the side of the American family would reconsider and so allay the concerns of the American public. But I'm afraid there's little hope of that."

More calls from the press, and Senator Wickham held up his hand for quiet.

Cooper felt himself sweating, as if he had just come off a nine-mile cross run.

"Here is the story as we have pieced it together: Fourteen years ago, before the President and First Gentleman were married, they checked into Keene Memorial Hospital and there had a son, this boy, Cooper Jewett. They hoped that the birth of the child would never be known."

Notes being scribbled wildly by the reporters. Cooper blinked away the dazzling still in his eyes.

"They gave the child to their secretary, Eustachius Bolster, who abandoned him at a farm in New Lincoln, where the boy was raised as Cooper Jewett by Eli and Edna Jewett. As far as we know, Mr. and Mrs. Jewett were innocent in all of this. They never knew who the boy's parents really were. But from that day to this, there have been rumors about the boy in New Lincoln and in Washington."

"But what proof, Senator?" called a reporter. "Are there any records?"

"The President and First Gentleman tried to ensure that there were none. But one set of records did survive." He held up the folder. "This folder holds the birth certificate and medical records of Cooper Bradford, or Jewett, as he is now called. As to the identity of his parents, there are witnesses." He pointed to the front row. "Three witnesses. The attending physician and the two nurses present at the birth. In the congressional hearings sure to follow this press meeting, subpoenas will be issued to these and others, including neighbors of the Jewett family, the President and First Gentleman, and Mr. Eustachius Bolster, the President's private secretary and, we believe, the man who delivered the child to the Jewett farm fourteen years ago." He took a glossy photograph out of the folder. "We can see that Mr. Bolster has maintained an interest in Cooper."

Cooper couldn't see the photograph, but he was sure that it had been taken of the two of them the night before in the barn.

"It's a blurry print," said a reporter. "Could be anyone."

"Cooper will confirm Mr. Bolster's identity," said Senator Wickham.

Cooper felt as if he were on stage and he couldn't

remember his lines. He didn't even know if he was supposed to have any lines. He really did think he might throw up. The coffee in his stomach seemed to be churning around and around and around. He didn't exactly want to throw up in front of a room full of reporters and cameras. But then, if he had to throw up, he knew where he'd aim.

He wished with a powerful wish that Mr. Searle and Mrs. Perley were there. And the Hurds. Peter. But he remembered what his grandfather had said. *The good Lord isn't just going to send something along because you wished for it.*

But his grandfather had been wrong.

Because then, just as it sometimes happens in dreams, the wish became real, and there was Peter standing at the back of the room, standing—yes, he really was—standing on a chair and waving at him. And there was Mrs. Hurd, her hand on the Reverend Hurd's shoulder, and next to him stood Mr. Searle—which was probably about as close as Mr. Searle had ever come to a reverend in his whole life. And in front of all four, her hands up to her cheeks, stood Mrs. Perley.

They all blurred together, maybe because Cooper was so tired he could hardly see or maybe because of something else. He stood, and immediately the Very Big Man laid a hand on his shoulder.

"Senator, are you detaining this boy?" called out a reporter.

"You're darn tootin'," came a voice from the back. Mr. Searle.

"Hey, Cooper, are you here because you want to be?" asked another reporter.

Even standing behind Senator Wickham, Cooper could see him start to sweat. He shifted back and forth.

"Of course, I have no legal authority to hold Cooper," said Senator Wickham slowly. "The boy is here of his own will to right a terrible wrong. And as a citizen and Senator of these United States, I have a moral authority to help represent the truth." He pointed at Cooper. "And the truth resides with this boy." He turned and looked at Cooper, then turned back to the microphone again. "A boy who should, finally, after all these years, find out for himself the reality of his parentage. A boy who has lived with cows, mucking out their stalls—good Lord—while he should have been sleeping in the White House."

It was right then that Cooper felt the reporters starting to turn against Senator Wickham. He could feel it in the new silence in the room. He could see it in the way their eyes darkened. After all, many of these reporters were from New Hampshire, and almost every single one of them had farming deep in the blood. A lot had mucked out stalls all their childhood. And it seemed as if the dearest farming traditions of their state had just been insulted.

The Very Big Man felt it too. He tightened his hand on Cooper's shoulder.

If Senator Wickham felt it, he gave no sign. He leaned down over the podium to the witnesses in the first row.

"Dr. Thatcher," said Senator Wickham, "you have a statement."

The doctor stood up slowly, and Cooper could see that he was as nervous as all get-out. He took his hands out of his pockets, then put them back in and took them out again. He took his glasses off. He coughed lightly twice. He put his glasses back on.

"We'll follow Dr. Thatcher's statement with questions," said Senator Wickham. "Dr. Thatcher?"

Dr. Thatcher nodded, then hesitantly walked along the front of the platform. Slowly he climbed up the six stairs, looking as if Senator Wickham were a hangman waiting for him by the gallows.

Cooper watched him with unblinking eyes.

This man had seen the moment of his birth.

This man had seen his parents.

Maybe.

"Ladies and gentlemen of the press, I introduce to you Dr. James Thatcher, head of obstetrics at Keene Memorial Hospital. Fourteen years ago, Dr. Thatcher was the physician on call on the date that Mr. and Mrs.

Hugh Bradford came to the hospital to deliver their son. Dr. Thatcher."

Dr. Thatcher had finally finished climbing the stairs to the podium. Cooper thought that now he wasn't the only one in the room who looked ready to throw up. Dr. Thatcher had taken his hands out of his pockets— no, now they were back in—and his mouth was working as if he were chewing.

Senator Wickham stepped away from the podium and smiled.

Dr. Thatcher approached the microphone. His eyes moved, searching across the room.

"Dr. Thatcher," said Senator Wickham.

Slowly Dr. Thatcher leaned down over the microphone. His lips opened, and closed.

Silence in the room still.

Dr. Thatcher opened his mouth again, and finally spoke: "Ladies and gentlemen of the press, ladies and gentlemen . . ." He paused, took a deep breath, and began again. "Ladies and gentlemen, it is with regret that, speaking both for Nurses Stoneham and Culver and myself, I must inform you of an enormous misunderstanding." He swallowed.

If the room had been silent when Cooper walked in, suddenly it was soundless.

Senator Wickham's eyes closed to slits as Dr.

Thatcher leaned forward and spoke quickly, as if he had rehearsed his piece and could hardly wait to be done with it.

"We deliver, on average, seven hundred and forty children each year at Keene Memorial Hospital. On such a busy ward, it would be impossible for any one doctor or nurse to remember with perfect clarity a patient and child who came to the hospital fourteen years ago, particularly in the case of an uneventful birth. Certainly, in a case with implications as momentous as this one, none of us are willing to identify positively a Mr. and Mrs. Hugh Bradford or to suggest that the First Gentleman and President are that couple. As to the young man in question here, without DNA testing of both the parents and the child, no one can confirm their genetic connection beyond a doubt." Dr. Thatcher looked down at Cooper. "I'm sorry, but I cannot tell you who your parents might have been."

The silence ended as the reporters erupted. Cameras flashed again, and the doctor held up his hand against the bright lights.

But Cooper wasn't watching the doctor. He was watching Senator Wickham, and what was in his eyes was not peace and joy and love.

And Cooper—Lord forgive him—smiled just a bit.

Senator Wickham did not smile back. He walked to

the podium and turned to the doctor, who almost seemed to tremble.

"Two days ago, Doctor, you positively identified Mr. and Mrs. Hugh Bradford as the First Gentleman and President of the United States. Positively. Just two days ago."

"I am afraid, Senator, you took my willingness to appear here and to address questions about hospital routine as confirmation."

"You're afraid. What are you afraid of, Doctor? Afraid of the truth? Or afraid of speaking the truth? Who's gotten to you? The President?" Senator Wickham turned back to the press. "Ladies and gentlemen . . ." He looked around him, saw Cooper, and turned to him. "Your farm is on the line now," he whispered, as he motioned for the Very Big Man to lead Dr. Thatcher away, and leaned in to the microphone.

"Ladies and gentlemen, let me introduce you to the young man himself."

Senator Wickham gestured for Cooper to come stand beside him, and Cooper came. Once again the reporters' cameras flashed. Senator Wickham put his arm along Cooper's shoulders.

"This is Cooper Jewett, who was abandoned by the President and First Gentleman. He is only now learning of his past—it has been hidden from him very effectively— but he may be able to answer some questions. Yes, Hannah."

Hannah Joyce stood up. Hannah Joyce herself! *So she is going to report about me after all,* thought Cooper.

"Cooper," she said, "are you aware that this morning, papers were filed on your behalf to make Mrs. Sarah Perley your legal guardian?"

"What?" said Senator Wickham.

"And," continued Hannah Joyce, "that a second set of papers have been filed to make Mr. Farnham Searle the legal trustee of your farm, to hold in trust for you until your eighteenth birthday? Were you aware of this, Cooper?"

Cooper shook his head.

"Cooper, has anyone in the America for Wickham campaign threatened you or your farm if you did not cooperate with them?"

Senator Wickham stood stunned—only for a second. He leaned down again to the microphone. "Ms. Joyce, the implication that—"

"Yes," said Cooper loudly.

"—that my campaign would stoop to tactics such as—"

"Do you know if you are the President's son?" asked Hannah Joyce.

Everyone in the room stilled. Even Senator Wickham. And Cooper felt himself grow light, and when he looked at Reverend Hurd and Mrs. Hurd and Peter, and Mrs. Perley and Mr. Searle, he almost laughed out loud.

"I'm Cooper Jewett," he said. "I'm not the President's

son. But I am a fine runner, I have fine friends, and I'm a moderate driver. I am a Methodist most Sundays. I am a dairyman every day. And I live with people who . . . people who love me."

And he jumped down off the stage.

★ ★ ★ ★ ★ ★ ★ ★ ★

# CHAPTER TEN

By THE TIME Cooper hit the floor, it felt like there were little carbonated bubbles rushing through his bloodstream, ready to bust in his heart. But his heart was too full to bust.

Cameras were pushed in front of him and flashes popped in his face as reporters called and the abandoned Senator Wickham watched from the podium. Cooper even saw Hannah Joyce herself angling toward him. This is what it would be like to be on a campaign, he thought. This is what it would be like if I lived in the White House.

Suddenly there was Peter, punching him on the arm. "A fine runner?" he said.

And there were the Hurds beside him. And Mrs. Perley stretching her arms around him as far as they could go.

And Mr. Searle standing next to them all and finally reaching out and tousling Cooper's hair.

"Time to go," he said to Cooper. "Morning milking's done but not the mucking out."

"Thanks," said Cooper.

"And don't expect the Methodist parson to do it proper."

Cooper shook his head.

"Or me to do evening milking all alone."

Cooper shook his head again, ready to laugh, to laugh out loud with the hilarious joy of mucking out proper.

"Then let's go home," said Mrs. Perley.

So with Peter and the Hurds in front and Mr. Searle and Mrs. Perley behind, Cooper began to push through the reporters, while cameras still flashed and hands still waved. Above them all, Cooper heard the voice of the stricken Senator Wickham, and he smiled. He figured that the Senator hadn't had things go quite the way he wanted.

But things didn't go quite the way Cooper wanted either. The reporters jammed around them so that they could hardly move. Cooper wasn't all that surprised when, before he got to the door, he felt a hand as big as a shovel grab on to his shoulder, and then another hand grasp his other shoulder. He felt the hands spin him, and he was staring into the chest of the Very Big Man. Beside him stood Senator Wickham.

But Cooper was surprised when Mr. Searle shouted, "Get out of the boy's way," and when he twirled the Very Big Man around and, with all the strength of a New Hampshire plow, pulverized the Very Big Man's nose.

A cry of pain. Reporters standing and yelling, and chairs toppling backward. More cameras flashing.

Mrs. Perley took Cooper's arm. But Senator Wickham grabbed him too and leaned close, his face red and stretched. Cooper could almost smell the fury. "Say good-bye to your farm," he whispered fiercely.

"Say good-bye to your campaign," said Cooper.

"Not yet," said Senator Wickham.

Then Mr. Searle was next to them both, and he was holding up his bloody knuckles and looking about as fierce as a New Hampshire dairyman can look. Senator Wickham backed away, then he forced on a smile for the reporters.

With Mr. Searle beside them holding up his knuckles, they pushed through the cameras and recorders. Every reporter in the press room moved aside at the sight of the knuckles. "It was like," Reverend Hurd said later, "the Red Sea parting again and Mr. Searle leading us away from the Egyptian host."

Outside the hotel entrance, in a place marked "For Official Business Only," Sheriff Gibbs's patrol car waited.

"Get in," said a smiling Mrs. Perley.

"This'll be frightening," said Mr. Searle to Cooper.

"It's the sheriff's car," said Cooper.

"Bolster gave it to her last night. She hasn't been the same since."

Cooper looked at the Hurds, who were grinning. "She promised to give all the kids rides on Sunday," said Mrs. Hurd.

Cooper climbed onto the front seat between Mrs. Perley and Mr. Searle. The Hurds got in the back. "Buckle up," Mrs. Perley said, and she flipped on the red lights, set the sirens screaming, ran the patrol car backward and half onto the sidewalk across the street, and sped out into the road. Cars cleared ahead of them, and they were on the highway in less than a minute.

They were going something above ninety miles an hour almost all the way home.

They all screamed with delight at each swerve.

They took the exit to New Lincoln on two wheels and flashed through town so fast that Cooper could just barely make out Sheriff Gibbs on the sidewalk, shaking his fist at them.

Mrs. Perley stopped at New Lincoln Methodist to drop off the Hurds—"Safe by grace alone," said Reverend Hurd—and then they were skidding in the gravel of Cooper's driveway.

"That is driving," she said.

"That's illegal," said a breathless Mr. Searle.

"It is not illegal to speed in a patrol car, you old fuddy-dud," said Mrs. Perley, and they got out.

Cooper breathed in all the smells around him. Out in the Far Pasture the cows were chomping. In the Orchard, the bare apple trees were only dreaming about budding out. The chicken coop needed a coat of white paint. Maybe next spring he'd get some hatchlings.

If he still had a farm next spring.

Cooper shivered when he thought of Senator Wickham's face so close to his own. *Say good-bye to your farm.*

Mr. Searle and Mrs. Perley came up beside him. "There's still the mucking out to do," said Mr. Searle.

"You will do the mucking out," said Mrs. Perley, "and the evening milking too. Cooper was up all night."

"I can do it," said Cooper.

"The old buzzard can do it," said Mrs. Perley. "You get some sleep. Whatever would your grandmother say?"

So Cooper went to his room and fell asleep, and though he did mean to be up for evening chores, he only awoke halfway through them. So when he came into the Big Barn, Mr. Searle and Mrs. Perley were milking side by side, fussing at each other—"Are you going to wash that blood off your knuckles, or are you going to keep it for a prize?"—and then Cooper was with them, and they were all laughing at the bloody knuckles, and everything in the Big Barn was warm and safe.

★ 183 ★

All through evening milking, everything was warm and safe. All through the early news, which featured some spectacular footage of Cooper's leap off the stage. All through supper, which they had together in Cooper's kitchen. All through tidying up. Everything was warm and safe.

Until deep night.

*Say good-bye to your farm,* Senator Wickham had warned.

Cooper decided to keep watch.

He figured there was no way in creation that Mrs. Perley would let him, so at eight he told her he was going to bed. Which he did for a little while. Then he put on a cross sweatshirt and coat and climbed out of his window (he was getting good at these escapes) onto the porch roof, from there to the railing, and then to the ground. He looked into the kitchen window and saw Mrs. Perley and Mr. Searle sitting beside each other, sipping tea. Then he went out to the Big Barn.

He stroked each of his cows as they settled down into the cold darkness. He could tell that Moon and Star were glad to have him home. They mooed gently and swayed their great heads back and forth whenever he came close. They almost cuddled up to him when he put his hands on their sides. Then he settled into a stack of hay bales by the far barn door.

He dozed.

He dozed for a long time and dreamed dreams he could not remember, only feel.

And then he heard Moon and Star, restless in their stalls, and he was no longer dozing.

The sound of a can on the cement of the barn floor. Cooper reached for the light switch.

Something pouring, and more of the cows waking up and mooing. And Cooper threw on the electric and hollered like Beelzebub.

The lights, the hollering, the bellowing of the cows, and the screech of Sheriff Gibbs all came at the same moment, and Sheriff Gibbs never expected any of them. He leaped into something that seemed safe, but he chose a stall that Cooper had not mucked out during chores. When he stood up, he was covered in something no one likes to be covered in and holding the gasoline can he had dropped. Gas had spilled all around him.

He took out a book of matches from his pocket.

"So, the First Boy himself." He tried to say it menacingly, but it's hard to be menacing when you're covered with fresh cow muck.

"You're in my barn, Sheriff Gibbs."

"It won't be here tomorrow. And neither will you be. You'll be far away, in a place for homeless orphans."

"By tomorrow, Mrs. Perley will be my legal guardian."

"Don't count on it. Those things can get delayed for a long time. Paperwork lost, committees stalled." He shook his head. "Don't you get it? All you had to do was sit there. That's all you had to do. The President would have resigned from the campaign, and you'd have parents again—not that they'd be too glad about it. But you'd have been all set."

"And you'd be a bureau chief in Washington, D.C."

"And I'd be a bureau chief in Washington, D.C."

"Instead you don't even have your patrol car."

Sheriff Gibbs narrowed his eyes. "So smart, aren't you? So dang smart. The Senator asked me to give you a present. He wanted to be sure you knew who it was from."

He held the match over the pool of gasoline. The cows mooed at the new smell.

Now Sheriff Gibbs *was* menacing, and Cooper looked wildly around him. How would he get the cows out?

"You won't be able to stop it," said the sheriff. "You'll lose the cows or the barn. Maybe both."

"Everyone will know you set the fire."

"Funny thing about that, Cooper. You see, I'm actually over at America for Wickham campaign headquarters. This very second. The Senator himself will swear to it if any questions are asked. Folks will figure there's been another fire over at the Jewett place, and, my, my, but that boy who lives over there shouldn't be allowed to stay where who knows what will happen next."

Cooper thought he might cry.

The sheriff struck the match.

"No!" shouted Cooper.

Sheriff Gibbs smiled above his considerable chin and dropped the match.

Just as a flash of light came from the barn door.

And Hannah Joyce ran in.

She stopped and flashed another picture of the fleeing sheriff.

The flames caught the hay.

"The cows!" called Cooper. "Get the cows!" But Hannah Joyce ran back outside.

Desperate, Cooper grabbed Moon, her eyes big and frightened. He tugged and screamed and finally got her running out. He grabbed Star, and she followed Moon. But when he pulled at the next cow, she bellowed and stiffened her legs. Cooper ran to the next stall and tugged, but this cow was just as stiff. Cooper yanked at her hopelessly.

Then Hannah Joyce came running back in with a fire extinguisher. She pulled the pin and began to spray. "Get the other bales away before they catch!" she yelled.

Cooper ran from the stall and began to throw bales away from the flames, but soon the heat of the fire was too intense to get close, and even though the extinguisher had stopped the fire from spreading on the floor of the barn, the flames were licking up the posts and against the loft.

Then the extinguisher ran out.

"We've got to get the cows!"

"You start down there," Hannah Joyce cried. She did not even stop to take a picture.

Cooper dragged two more cows from their stalls and out the barn, but Hannah Joyce couldn't manage even one.

And then suddenly there was Mrs. Perley, and Mr. Searle came running—dressed in his pajamas.

"Get on the Farmall," he called.

"No," said Cooper. He didn't care if they lost the tractor. He had to get the cows out.

Mr. Searle ran out, and soon he'd backed the Farmall close to the barn door. He gunned the engine so that it could be heard above the snapping of the flames. And then he started from the barn.

The cows strained to follow. Cooper and Mrs. Perley and Hannah Joyce ran from stall to stall and released the tethers, and immediately the cows almost galloped after the Farmall.

By the time the cows had left, smoke had filled the Big Barn. Hannah Joyce ran out, coughing and trying to take pictures at the same time. Cooper pulled Mrs. Perley out after her. "There's two still to get," he called, turning back.

"Cooper, let them go," cried Mr. Searle from the barn door.

But Cooper ignored him. He ran low to the floor, just

beneath the hot blue-black smoke, and reached the last two stalls. Half standing, he jerked the tethers from the cows, but they were so frightened they wouldn't move.

"Sorry," he said, and stuck his fingers as far up their nostrils as he could reach. The cows bellowed and reared, but Cooper held on and stepped back, and they followed. Step by step out of the burning barn he went, feeling more than seeing his way. And then Mr. Searle was there, grabbing one by the ear, smacking out the sparks that fell on Cooper's shoulders, until finally they were outside. The cows, shaking their heads, rushed to the Near Pasture to join the others, and Hannah Joyce, Mr. Searle, Cooper, and Mrs. Perley stood together, the heat of the fire blasting the cold air.

"Well," said Hannah Joyce, breathless, "well." She took some pictures of the barn to steady herself, changed rolls, and took some more.

"Stuck your fingers up into their snot," said Mr. Searle.

"Learned it from a smart neighbor," said Cooper. "I didn't know about the Farmall."

"Cows always follow a tractor. They think it's carting hay."

"Do you always wear bright red pajamas?" said Mrs. Perley.

"No," said Mr. Searle. "Usually I'm in the altogether, Sarah Perley. What do you think about that?"

"That it is fortunate for all humanity that you live alone."

Now the fire suddenly curled around the edges of the roof, its flames a bright blue, and within hardly a second the roof was ablaze, draped in horrid light.

Mrs. Perley put her hands on Cooper's shoulders. "You saved all the cows," she said. "Your grandparents would have been so proud."

But Cooper did not feel proud. The cows were saved, but the milking equipment was gone. Everything he needed to make the farm prosper would be burned to ashes or warped in the heat of the flames.

"I'm so sorry for you, Cooper," said Hannah Joyce. "Where will you put the cows?"

"They'll stay in my barn," said Mr. Searle. "If Cooper wants them there, that is."

Cooper nodded. Where else? "Thanks," he said quietly.

Hannah Joyce took one last picture. "It may be that the barn is gone," she said, "but I heard everything the sheriff said, and I have the pictures. All of New Hampshire will hear about it. I'll put the whole story on the morning news and send the pictures out over the wires."

And she did.

The next morning, when Cooper came back from milking and from driving Mr. Searle's cows and his own cows out into the pasture, the newspaper was waiting in the mailbox. The photo of Sheriff Gibbs took up a quarter of the page and ran beneath a bold headline:

SHERIFF GIBBS BURNS DOWN JEWETT BARN,
SENATOR WICKHAM IMPLICATED.

By the afternoon edition, which Mrs. Perley brought over, Senator Wickham had denied any connections, but Sheriff Gibbs was handing over notes about Cooper Jewett, directions about burning the Small Barn to drive Cooper off the farm and set up a distraction, a letter about Mr. Searle—all in the Senator's hand.

By the evening news, which Cooper heard at Mr. Searle's when he went down for milking, Hannah Joyce was announcing a coming congressional hearing, at which Sheriff Gibbs would be the star attraction. "Looks like he'll make it to Washington, D.C., after all," said Mr. Searle, and bit into a raspberry tart.

Senator Wickham knew more about working Congress than anyone else alive, so he had the congressional hearing delayed until after Christmas and then delayed again for another four weeks so he could confer with someone or other. But in the end, it didn't much matter. When the New Hampshire primary came in January, Senator Wickham hardly got enough votes to fill a hat. The count was announced early in the morning, and Senator Wickham resigned from the race before the six o'clock news even thought of beginning. "I am disappointed that I was not able to get my message across," he said.

Throughout that winter, Mr. Searle and Cooper milked their cows together and drove them out and then back from the pasture. And when the last cow was settled, they closed the barn doors and climbed up to Cooper's farm, where Mrs. Perley was watching for them from the window of Cooper's kitchen. She cooked breakfasts and suppers that weren't interested in keeping a cross country runner at his weight.

And last thing at night, Cooper walked around his farm, even though there were no barns to check and no shed to pull the Farmall in under. But there were still a hundred and sixty acres of rolling land, and Cooper never tired of looking at them—especially at night, when he couldn't see the gaps of the missing barns. It was a winter when it seemed to snow lightly almost every afternoon, just before dark. Then the sky would clear, and the moon would come up. When Cooper walked out, he could hardly breathe for the glittering light that sparkled in the meadows. The bare arms of the apple trees in the Orchard gleamed silver.

About a week after the fire, Cooper began receiving letters with checks from people he didn't even know who had read Hannah Joyce's wire report. From people who didn't even live in New Hampshire! Sometimes there was a note saying that the money should go to rebuilding the two barns. Sometimes there was just the check. "Oh, my gracious goodness," said Mrs. Perley when she saw the pile of them. "What will you do with it all?"

"First, pay Mr. Searle what Grandpa owed. Then the barns."

Mr. Searle would have none of it, but Cooper insisted.

In March, Mr. Searle came up with blueprints for the new barns, and Mrs. Perley drove them to the New Lincoln Lumberyard in her patrol car, sirens screaming and red lights blinking all the way. "You need to make an entrance," she said. While they waited for the lumber to be delivered, Mrs. Hurd organized the congregation of New Lincoln Methodist, and on the first warm and lovely Saturday of the spring, when the bees had woken up and the apple trees were no longer dreaming, they all met to raise a Small Barn and a Big Barn on the Jewett dairy farm.

Hannah Joyce came out to report for the six o'clock news.

They had the two frames up by noon, and Cooper, Peter, and everyone else from New Lincoln Methodist were just sitting down to Reverend Hurd's prayer and a picnic lunch when a jeep drove up. It was Bolster. He waited for Cooper on the driveway.

With a dog.

A dog who bounded out of the jeep with its legs going all over and its tongue hanging out and its tail heading every way. It ran through Cooper's legs, came around and did it again, and came around again and jumped up at him.

"It's a retriever," said Bolster.

Cooper bent down and put his face against the dog's. The dog licked him as fast as it could.

"It likes you, kid. Either that or you taste good."

Cooper looked up at Bolster through the licking. "Is he for me?"

"She," said Bolster. "Take Biology after you finish World Cultures. And she's for you. She looks like she'll be all sorts of trouble. You were made for each other."

The dog finished licking him and started to eat his shoelaces, while Cooper rubbed his hands into the gold coat.

"You'll need a name," Bolster said.

"I've already got one," said Cooper.

Bolster shook his head. "I'm not surprised. Now, kid, I have a message for you from the President and First Gentleman." Cooper nodded. "They want me to tell you they admire and respect you. They promise that no one will ever try to take you off the farm. And they hope you have a happy life."

Cooper looked around his farm, at the two new barns going up, at the cows in the Far Pasture, and at Mrs.

Perley and Mr. Searle, holding hands and watching him. He felt rhythm deep down inside, and if there was an ache too, it wasn't a bad ache. Maybe the hole in his heart was filling in all the way. Or at least, filling in as much as anyone's heart is ever filled in.

"Tell them," he said, "I wish the same for them."

Bolster nodded.

"And I have a message from me too, kid."

Cooper smiled. "What?"

"I've driven through swamps in Burma, across deserts in North Africa, and straight up mountains in Tibet. And I've always figured that there wasn't anyone else who could do the same. Then I met you."

Bolster smiled and shook Cooper's hand. "You got guts, kid. Real guts. I've got one more thing for you." He took an envelope from his pocket and handed it to him. "Open it."

Cooper took out two tickets. He looked at Bolster. "Peru?"

"I'm taking you to Machu Picchu, kid. The week after you finish school."

"You are?"

"Who else, kid?"

And Cooper nodded. Of course. Who else?

"If you ever want to live on a dairy farm," said Cooper, "I know someone who's got one. But you'd need a different suit."

Bolster looked at him, his face a little crooked, and that was when Cooper saw that Bolster knew too: Sometimes, talking is only silence that ain't working well. And the silence between them said enough. Bolster got back into his jeep. Waving, he drove off. He drove off slowly.

With Barkus's tail thumping the ground beside him, Cooper watched until the jeep took the turn to New Lincoln and was gone.

By late afternoon, the Small Barn was up and the Big Barn was framed—mostly because of Mr. Searle, who taught Cooper how to work the handsaw smoothly and how to hammer straight every time, without bending a nail to kingdom come. But mostly he sent Cooper and Peter to play with the dog, which they did. In fact, they messed around with her most of the afternoon, and no one—not even Mr. Searle—fussed at them.

The day settled into tired quietness, and the congregation of New Lincoln Methodist left, singing "Bringing in the Sheaves," which they thought appropriate to the situation. They'd be back next weekend to finish the Big Barn. Cooper waved them over the hill in the darkening light. Then he walked back up to the house, where Mrs. Perley and Mr. Searle sat together on the top porch step—which had stopped groaning somehow—holding hands. Barkus set to work right away on their shoelaces.

"Is everything all right?" asked Mrs. Perley.

"All right," said Cooper.

He went inside and sprawled on the parlor couch. Barkus followed him in. She sniffed a bit, circled four or five times, and then dropped into a golden heap in the middle of the floor. She was asleep in hardly a second, her back legs kicking out now and again.

Cooper lay for a long time on the couch, looking across at his grandmother's rocker, at his grandfather's desk. It wasn't hard at all to see them sitting there. Maybe they wouldn't have minded Barkus in the house. Well, maybe they would have. But even so, Cooper couldn't hear them scolding him. He could only hear them say something else: *You're our first boy, Cooper, our first boy.*

*I'll always have them,* he thought.

It was enough. More than enough.

He yawned and stretched, then stood. He woke up Barkus. There was evening milking to get to. The cows would be waiting for him.

# GOFISH

## questions for the author

**GARY SCHMIDT**

**What did you want to be when you grew up?**
I wanted to go into the navy. Then I wanted to become a vet. Sometimes, I still want to become a vet.

**When did you realize you wanted to be a writer?**
Not until graduate school. I was working on a dissertation, and a lot of it was in Latin; and one night I was so sick of it that I could hardly stand it. So I started a children's book, and it stunk, but I enjoyed writing it. That was when I was about twenty-six or so. I was not one of those kids you meet so often who know they want to be writers and have poems and keep journals, and work for the school newspaper.

**What's your first childhood memory?**
A spider that a kid drew in kindergarten. Somehow, whenever I think of my first memory, that's it. The kid's name was Glen Sweiteck, and our teacher, Mrs. Hershey, hung the picture on the wall. I remember being frightened by it because it was so scary. That was my first encounter with art.

**What's your most embarrassing childhood memory?**
Probably throwing a gallon of bright yellow oil paint on my brother. It was impossible to get out, and it was in his hair and everywhere.

**As a young person, who did you look up to most?**
Probably my grandmother. Her name was Gertrude Smith. She was an amazing reader, a wonderful storyteller, and a very calm and pacific person. I went to the library first with her. She got me an adult library card when I was ten.

**What was your worst subject in school?**
When I was young, reading was my worst subject. We were divided into groups very early on and, though they gave us innocuous names, I was in the pumpkin group, and knew that was the worst. We were always 2-3 books behind the best readers—and we were constantly reminded of that. Later, a teacher named Ms. Kabikoff made me read, and introduced me to a lot of wonderful books. I read some books that were too easy for me, but she let me read them, and that gave me the confidence to try older books. If it weren't for her, I probably wouldn't be a reader. And no one can be a writer who isn't a reader first.

**What was your first job?**
I washed dishes for a Presbyterian church; it was $6 an evening. After that, I worked up at a camp, also washing dishes, landscaping, cleaning pools. I hated cleaning pools.

**How did you celebrate publishing your first book?**
I remember I was doing advising days, getting a student every fifteen minutes, and in the middle of that, Virginia called. I said, "Hey, Virginia, what's up?" thinking it was a student. And then I realized who it was, and I said, "Is this

'the' Virginia Buckley?" and she said, "This is 'a' Virginia Buckley." But we didn't really celebrate.

**Where do you write your books?**
We have a small outbuilding, outside the house, one of the early buildings on the farm we live on. The roof was falling in when we moved in and, since the house was built in 1837, we decided we would use tools from only that period to rebuild it. The books and my desk are there; it's heated with an old, wood-burning stove. I type on a 1953 Royal typewriter.

**Where do you find inspiration for your writing?**
I'm always a little leery of the word inspiration because it seems to suggest that an idea comes from on high and hovers above like a muse. I think the word I'd rather use is "awake." I think all writers need to be awake to the moments that you feel will lead to a story. When you come upon that idea, you recognize it as a potential story—which sounds easier than it is.

**Which of your characters is most like you?**
I think on some level, they all are. In *First Boy,* I think that Cole is a lot like me. In *The Wednesday Wars,* Holling is closest to my own experience. In *Lizzy Bright and the Buckminster Boy,* Turner is the kid I would have ideally liked to have been. Cole is living the way I would have liked to live, on a farm with tractors.

**When you finish a book, who reads it first?**
My wife, Anne. But she doesn't read it until it's completely finished, and we don't even talk about it until it's completely finished. I think if you talk about a book, you diffuse the energy of writing it. You're in the process of discovery as you

write; if you talk it through, all of it is gone. You've worked it out, expressed it. That's why I'm not a part of a writers' group.

**Are you a morning person or a night owl?**
Definitely morning. At 9:00 P.M., I'm in bed.

**What's your idea of the best meal ever?**
Any meal that ends with my wife's apple pie. It really doesn't matter what comes before.

**Which do you like better: cats or dogs?**
Dogs. No human being really likes cats. People just say they do because they feel sorry for them. Cats can't like anyone because they're so arrogant. You always know what a dog's thinking, what they're about to do. There's something generous about a dog.

**What do you value most in your friends?**
Loyalty, hard work, a shared commitment to a redemption of the culture.

**Where do you go for peace and quiet?**
Home.

**What makes you laugh out loud?**
Really good writing, a clever handling of language. It comes so rarely, and hardly ever comes in the media, but when it comes, it's perfect. There used to be a show called *Brooklyn Bridge* by Gary Goldberg about kids growing up in the 1950s, one family was Jewish, the other Roman Catholic. The guy from the first family falls in love with Mary in the second family, and all of the situations arise from

those complications. I loved it. *The West Wing* is also brilliantly done.

**What's your favorite song?**
Beethoven's Ninth Symphony.

**Who is your favorite fictional character?**
The one that pops to mind is Oliver from Oliver Twist. I think he's a brilliant character by Dickens. Also the warden in Anthony Trollope's books. He's a sweet, sweet guy, the archetypal vision of sweet. But if I had to pick just one, I'd go with Oliver Twist.

**What are you most afraid of?**
A fear that something ill might happen to my children.

**What time of the year do you like best?**
Winter. To walk out when the moon is out after a freshly fallen snow, there is nothing like it. Or after the first frost when the sun is coming up.

**What is your favorite TV show?**
I don't watch any now. It's too depressing. And now with the notion of DVDs, you can watch without being interrupted every eight minutes.

**If you were stranded on a desert island, who would you want for company?**
My wife.

**If you could travel in time, where would you go?**
Revolutionary Boston. I would like to have seen that. Can you imagine it? The beginning of a new country.

**What's the best advice you have ever received about writing?**
Eighth grade, Mr. Shamsky, "Show, don't tell." It's a cliché now, and you hear it in every single writing class, but that was the first time I'd heard it. I can even hear his voice as he spoke it and wrote it on the board.

**What do you want readers to remember about your books?**
That they're about hope. That they're about the notion that goodness is important and honor is important and nobility of purpose—all those are important. That it's important to grow up and not be lulled into a culture that says stay an adolescent because you're the best consumer when you're an adolescent. Turn your faces toward adulthood. You see commercials of four guys in their forties, sitting together drinking beer and watching the Super Bowl—and that's a good time? I'm thinking you act like that when you're twelve. It's a good time, but it's a time designed to end.

**What would you do if you ever stopped writing?**
I won't.

**What do you like best about yourself?**
I think I can be disciplined, and I think writing is all about discipline. It's not about waiting for inspiration or the muses or waiting to be an auteur. It's about sitting at your desk and getting your 2,000 words out.

**What is your worst habit?**
You probably should ask my wife that.

**What do you consider to be your greatest accomplishment?**
My six children.

**What do you wish you could do better?**
My six children.

**What would your readers be most surprised to learn about you?**
Probably that I write on a typewriter. In this day and age, where it's just assumed that you work on a computer, writing on a typewriter with a ribbon seems like something out of the Stone Age.